Of
LOVE
and
BRUISES

D1596543

BLESSING DOUGLAS

Fulton Books, Inc.
Meadville, PA

Published by Fulton Books 2021

ISBN 978-1-64952-046-3 (paperback)
ISBN 978-1-64952-047-0 (digital)

Printed in the United States of America

Dedication

....

This book is for all the children who had and are still having a traumatizing childhood.

For everyone moving around with physical and emotional scars stemming from abuse.

For all mental health survivors. Survivors who don't get a pat on their backs from anyone congratulating them for making it.

Survivors who wake up to more work and challenges because their friends and family are exhausted from helping them fight a battle they may not even understand.

I hope to one day see a sea of people attending more workshops, talking more, learning and loving as a sign that they understand the secret battle, and as a celebration of the victories made each day as we individually and collectively pull ourselves up out of our foxholes to see our scars heal and to remember what the sun looks like.

Looks like today is a good day to start.

acknowledgement

···

I want to thank everyone who inspired me to write this book.

I'm eternally grateful to Dr. Margee Ensign, Dr Lionel Von Frederick Rawlins, Jon Freeman, Byron Bullock, Ambassador Patrick Fay, Halima Sogbesan, Philip Eappen, Figgy Eappen, Bwama Fwa, Naomi Onyeomah, Onome Edeawe and Philip Somiari.

I truly have no idea where I'd be without your mentorship, support and encouragement.

Epigraph

....

Love is patient, love is kind. It does not boast, it is not proud. It does not dishonor others, it is not self-seeking, it is not easily angered, it keeps no record of wrongs.

1 Corinthians 13:4-5

Preface

....

While the bulk of this book is a collection of true stories, a few parts have been modified to protect identities while still passing the message across. Sadly, the issues discussed in this book is still the reality of so many children across the World.

The odd superstition and misinterpretation of bible verses "spare the rod and spoil the child" were all prevalent among parents and caregivers in Nigeria at the period of this story-It has been over two decades and not a lot has changed. Although my book is intended mainly to educate parents and care givers, I hope it will not be shunned by young adults and policy makers, for part of my plan has been to try to draw attention to the fact that physical abuse has consequences for both the abused and the society at large.

A 2020 WHO report states that "A child who is abused is more likely to abuse others as an adult so that violence is passed down from one generation to the next. It is therefore critical to break this cycle of violence, and in so doing create positive multi-generational impacts." Society should be concerned about creating and implementing policies that will achieve this. A failure to act, can hurt the nations human capital.

Alas It Was a Phantasy

"There is nothing ugly about you, Belema. You are like the rose petals that bloom in the morning. My dear, you are my rose petals. Every day I spend with you, I am reminded of how beautiful your mother is and how much she brought sunshine to my life." I sat between Grandma's legs as she combed my soft black hair. She loved making my hair. A soft wind swept into the room, causing the fire from the kerosene lamp to flicker. The silhouette of Grandma's face spread over the wall. Grandma scooped a dash of cream and rubbed it on my head. We were sitting on the two-seater sofa with patches sewn with black threads on both arms of the sofa. The night was young. Grandma and I had just finished eating dinner when she began her hairdressing work on me. She was good at it. Her hands were not as hard and painful as Iya Kemi's down the road.

"Mama, you always talk about my mother with so much love and light in your eyes. Why have I not seen her then? If she is so beautiful and caring and is such an angel, why hasn't she come for me all these years? Aren't you always saying that the love of a mother supersedes any love in the world? That a mother is God formed from the ocean? Always giving her love and never requiring the love of her child in return? Isn't it true that when a mother absolutely loves her child, the world can burn, and the Earth can pass away, but her child will remain crooned in her arms while she sings the child lullaby? Why hasn't my mother come for me all these years? If she is as caring and loving as a mother is supposed to be, why hasn't she come to see me?"

"Keep quiet and stop sounding like an ungrateful child, Belema." Grandma's voice rang with the firmness of an aged one and the subtlety of the wise. She never raised her voice at me whenever I started acting like a spoiled brat, asking questions and making statements that were too heavy for my childish tongue. She would only rebuke me not to burrow into holes I might never be able to bring myself out from. This night, however, her voice was not the same strong and soft one I was familiar with. This rebuke was harsher. She twisted my black hair in her hand, the neat weave she was making tightening my scalp. I was used to this tightness. It was soothing if you looked at it from the brighter side. Yes, there was bound to be headaches, which I always exaggerate because it affords me the chance to milk Mama of some bole (how I love those roasted fingers of plantain), fish, and Fanta. I love Fanta. Grandma said that if my husband comes to marry me, he would have to bring crates of Fanta to replace all the ones I have drank in her house.

"The trials of life aren't things you can logically explain," Grandma continued. Her voice took on the elderly softness I overheard her using for Papa Chidinma when he and his wife had a quarrel. "It is like the wind that blows: one day, it goes this way; the next day, it goes the other, confusing sailors on which route to follow. When you grow older, you'll understand the love of a mother and how sacrifices are necessary to sustain the one you love."

"Is it true that she is staying away because my father denied her pregnancy with me, or because she got married and didn't disclose my existence to her husband?" I asked Grandma. Grandma's voice became subdued. She stopped plaiting my hair. I could sense I had struck a nerve, said something I wasn't supposed to say.

After what felt like an hour but was only a few seconds, Grandma asked, "Where did you hear that, Belema?" At this point, I was quiet. "Your mum and dad were both very young when they had you. You should be grateful that your mother chose to keep you and not have an abortion."

"I heard she attempted to get rid of me a few times," I whispered under my breath. "I guess it was God's will for me to see the world."

Grandma heard me, but she ignored what I said and continued with her speech on why I shouldn't judge my parents so harshly.

I focused on her shadow reflected on the wall. I watched how her mouth moved in a swift motion as she spoke. How her head never left its position when she went into her deep philosophical lectures. On the night of this conversation, Grandpa was in Lagos, else he would have engaged her in her philosophical nonsense. See ehn, it is not like I don't like the talk o, but these people—Grandma and Grandpa—are fond of slipping into philosophy whenever they were talking to me. They think I have sense like that.

So one day when I went to the tap close to Mama Bruno's house to fetch water, I got into a fight with Suo. It was not like I was the one who really started the fight o. I was on my own, minding my business when Suo came from nowhere to accuse me of taking her chance. When I arrived at the tap, I only saw three boys and a girl there. The boys were huddled at one corner talking about Chelsea and Man U. I watched football with my grandpa sometimes, so I understood what they were talking about.

"That Chelsea coach doesn't know football. Who plays an inexperienced Tammy Abraham in such a big match?" I said as I came closer to the group. I dropped my green bucket behind the last yellow twenty-five-liters flagon before joining the boys.

"Abi, that coach na big fool o," one of the boys with a faded Chelsea jersey and red shorts torn at the side said. We were still talking about the third goal United scored and how Paul Pogba's pass was so good when Suo came with those big eyes of hers like oranges on the head of a sculptor and pushed my bucket away.

At first, I thought my eyes were deceiving me. But it wasn't. I walked briskly toward her. I was hoping beyond hope that she made a mistake by removing my bucket from the line. One of the boys was at the tap, and his third gallon was almost full.

"Suo, what is the problem? Why did you kick my bucket from the line? Did I place it on your head?" My voice was gentle as a sea. I did not raise my voice, even though the anger inside me was dancing skelewu. The anger had one hand on the waist and another on the chest, waiting to pounce on stupid Suo. The idiot girl that was seeing that ugly Femi boy behind the mango tree at night thinks she was the only one with a loose nut in the head. I was also crazy. I would show her what madness was.

"Are you mad? Have your ancestors from the ocean come on you today?" she yelled at me. The yellow spittle from her mouth fell on my face. I held myself from punching her in the face.

"Mad? You ask me if I am mad. What did I do?" I managed to say with all the calm I could muster.

"Didn't you meet my bucket here when you came?" she asked. I knew Suo liked trouble, but I never knew she went about igniting trouble at every whim.

I didn't know when my left hand raised itself and landed on her face. *Tawai.* I slapped her so hard, my palm started to hurt me. Before she could recover from that one, I gave her another. They say when you start a fight, ensure you are prepared to finish it. I was ready to fight.

I was still reveling in the hotness of my slap when I felt my leg leave the ground. Suo grabbed me and held me tightly against her stomach, the way a palm wine tapper knots his rope around a tree when climbing. She raised me up, and the next thing I knew, I was on the ground. My back slammed on the ground so hard, I thought my spinal cord was broken. With my back to the ground, Suo got on top of me, sat on my stomach, and started slapping me. She slapped me with both hands, alternating between two hits on each hand. When she got tired of slapping, she reached for the ground, packed a handful of sand, and started feeding me. The other children watched on, cheering Suo. That was the tradition here: Children watched fights with relish and cheered the winning fighter. As the tides of the fight changed, the cheers and loyalty switched.

When I got home after the pummeling Suo gave me, I was served a fresh dose of my grandparents' philosophical rambles. I call their talk rambles because I am often left with more questions than answers.

"You have to remember who you are," Grandpa was saying while Grandma massaged my back with a small towel soaked in hot water. I winced as she pressed the cloth on my back.

"Whose daughter, am I?" my mouth could not hold itself. I just had to ask.

"I will press your stupid mouth now if you don't keep quiet," Grandma threatened. Then she pressed the towel on my mouth.

"Belema, don't be quick to react all the time," Grandpa said. "Sometimes, be the fool so that peace will reign."

I stopped being the wise one whenever I was with them but be the fool? Never!

The memory of my grandparents' wise words took a back seat as Mama's hands tightened a line of cornrows. My scalp burned. I imagined the memory I had been playing with dashing off to the back of my head. I winced.

"I want to tell you something very important after I finish making your hair," Grandma said. Her voice didn't change one timbre. There was still that seriousness in her voice, the type that I had never heard before. We switched to pidgin English whenever I wanted to be naughty.

"Okay, Ma, but Grandma," I said with my fake teary voice, "I go like take Fanta when I finish o. This hair dey pain me well well."

"I know say na wetin you go talk. Every small thing, I want to take Fanta. Na Fanta naim go grow for your head. When you get to your father's house, use all his money to drink Fanta, you hear?"

"Shebi you talk say my papa get money?"

"As we don bring your papa matter enter so make I just tell you now before he too heavy for me later."

"Wetin happen to my papa?"

"Nothing bad. He is fine. He called me some days ago. Somiari wants you to come live with him. He feels he is settled now and should be responsible for you."

I felt like jolting from the ground and running around the house screaming at the top of my voice. Instead, I smiled like a newborn learning the art. The happiness spread over my heart like color over a sea. Then I started laughing.

My heart was pumped full of joy; it overflowed its banks. The thought of going to live with my father was exciting; I would enjoy it. He usually bought me toys whenever he came to see Grandpa and

Grandma. He was tall with black skin like charcoal. I liked him. His smile was always wide, like my grandpa's own. He took my granny's round face and flat nose, Grandpa's height, and booming voice. He walked like the lion I saw one day on Farah's phone: bold and confident. He walked with so much poise, so much confidence, it was hard not to call him a lion man.

After Grandma broke the news to me, I felt like riding on a flying horse. The kind of enjoyment I was going to be having ehn. By the time I returned from the city to the village during Christmas, all the village people go hail. I will show them that Belema is now a fine city girl. And not just any fine girl o, but this fine girl knows how to enjoy life to the fullest. I was even planning on sharing some of the toys and teddy bears he would buy for me with some of my friends when I returned for Christmas.

Granny was silent for the rest of the hair-plaiting session. She only said yes when I asked her if I could take the last bottle of Fanta in the fridge. She was acting as if I was going to a slaughterhouse.

"Grandma, wetin happen wey you quiet like person wey dem tiff him last card?" I gulped the chilled Fanta directly from the bottle. Then the electricity company, NEPA, restored power. It was typical of them, you know; always switching off power at the most important periods and bringing it back when less needed. I sat close to her on the threadbare three-seater couch. The threads on the couch were loosening, and the old foam was peering out from the couch like a shy kid.

"I will miss you a lot that is why I am quiet. Who would I talk to now? Who would ask me those random questions and finish my Fanta in the fridge?" Granny was teary. She hugged me. I allowed her tears to wash me clean before I started my new life with my amazing father. I wanted to tell Granny that I would bring crates of Fanta for her so she doesn't have to cry again. But I kept quiet. If Grandpa were there, he would have said I should let the words in my head form properly before I gave them passage through my mouth. I obeyed his wise words and just rested on Granny's shoulder while she cried away. My life was taking a new and glorious turn. Why was Granny crying? I will never understand these older adults, especially my grandmother.

Love with Sprinkles of Scoin Scoin

The wait for my dad's arrival was like the coming of Jesus. I waited with bated breath. My steps were infused with flash springs, and my eyes became home for the sun. I was always smiling. I walked around the village like the world was safely tucked in my panties. The swiftness with which I moved, the way I ran errands for Grandma, and how quick I was to break into a smile gave me away easily. My best friend, Dakumo, on the second day of my waiting, asked me why I was so happy.

"This one wey you dey ginger like this so wetin dey happen?"

I had planned on keeping my traveling away from everybody because I didn't want to jinx it. People in the village can be so jealous and diabolical. The jealousy can be so much that when they know that a good thing is about to happen to you or for you, they would do juju to stop you. That was how Dagogo, the boy whose mother sold akara down the street, did not travel to London again. Word had spread through his amebo friends that he would be traveling to London. He bragged to his friends that his mother would soon leave her akara business, and he would build her a big house. And that she would no longer wear her favorite cloth: green rapper with white horizontal stripes. The wrapper earned her the nickname, Mama Naija, from her customers.

A few days before he was to leave, Dagogo fell seriously sick. Nobody knew the cause of his sickness. Doctors and juju men were visited, nothing. Powerful men of God who sweated and shouted as they prayed for him in his squalid room did nothing to change his condition. He remained bedridden, unable to move a muscle. He could move his mouth, but words wouldn't come out. He automatically regained the use of his body parts two days after he was supposed to travel. When he went to the embassy to check if he could still travel, he misplaced his visa on his way back to the house. Mama Naija could not contain her anguish. Three months later, she sent her son to Lagos to save him from the shame and village rumors. Last I heard, Dagogo now smokes cannabis with Lagos touts and works as a bus conductor. The village people would not let him be.

I stared at Dakumo like she was talking gibberish. I knew telling her about my travelling was going to open a can of evil spirits, and bad belle people would start work on my head. We were in our sitting room that hot Saturday afternoon. Grandma had gone to the market to buy some things for my trip. Mama Aboy's grinding machine was making that gritting sound that made my skin crawl. Above the sound of the pepper grinding machine were the voices of Davo and Amaka. Those children can cry for Africa. They were doing their afternoon cry that rose higher than any noise you would hear on Ranpam Street. They were the street criers with their bloated stomachs and wide mouths.

"There is no special occasion. Can't one be happy again just because? Must there be an occasion for me to be happy?" I replied, trying my best to hide my blush. The thought of my dad and his house made me smile uncontrollably. I was helpless.

"Who is this one lying to? I know you very well, Belema, you can't just be happy for no reason." She moved closer to me, her face making inroads into my mind, searching for the secrets in the nearest corner of my head. She knew keeping secrets was one job I was awfully bad at.

She was close enough to me, her breathing so close to my face I was taking in her carbon dioxide while she was taking in mine. She looked into my eyes as if she was an older sister about to dish out some sagely wisdom. She knew how to get the words out of me.

"I have something to tell you," I said, blushing all over like a teenager newly in love. "No, tell anybody this thing wey I wan tell you now, na secret between us."

She smiled and kept quiet. I spilled the beans. She was super excited for me. Dakumo screamed and hugged me tightly. The yelp from Davo tore through our excitement. The grinding machine was off. Her body against mine, sweaty and sticky, like when Grandma rubbed shea butter on my skin when I had a hot water burn. The softness of it, the way it made all the hurt disappear as she applied it gently, whispering sweet pleas in my ears.

I promised Dakumo that I would bring her many toys and teddy bears when I returned to the village during Christmas. She also promised to keep our friendship till eternity.

"What should we do now to remember this friendship?" she inquired.

She scanned the room for something. There was nothing. I looked at her with awe as her eyes moved around the sitting room, looking for memorabilia of our friendship. I wanted to tell her that friendships were remembered best with sweet memories that we didn't need a physical thing to remind us of the person who pulls the strings of our hearts and made the world a burden less heavy to carry. I didn't need memorabilia. I had all the images of us together to keep the friendship alive, irrespective of distance.

She ran outside without saying a word. A few minutes later, she returned with two wristbands woven with black thread. Our names were inscribed into a small piece of wood woven in the middle of the wristbands. She gave me the one that had "Dakumo" engraved on it.

"Wear it," she said. "Whenever you feel alone, remember I am always here with you. And no go forget say I love you scatter." She put the wristband around my wrist. Hearing her say she loved me turned my heart into a leaping angel. I melted a thousand times. She wore the other wristband with my name on it and hugged me so tight, I thought I was going to meld into her.

My dad was to arrive the following day. I counted the minutes before the next day, too anxious to keep still. I could not help myself. Even when Grandma gave me my favorite Fanta and jollof rice, I could not finish it. I requested a pack of biscuits after I played with the food on my plate.

"Belema, this wan wey you no dey eat so. You sure say you fine?" Grandma was always asking questions she knew the answers to.

"I am fine, Grandma. I am too excited. I can't wait to see my father tomorrow," I replied.

Grandma smiled her weak smile. She was going to miss me badly. I knew it. But nothing beats living with your father and enjoying all the good things of life.

"Bele, make sure say you behave yourself tomorrow. When you get to your father's house"—she switched to English to indicate she was dead serious—"make sure you act like the good girl that you are. You should never forget the things we have taught you. Respect those older than you. Greet people. Say yes, sir, and yes, ma, to elders. Wake up early and do the house chores; you are a woman. Cook for your father, even if it's only rice you can boil. Wash his clothes. Make sure you clean his shoes." She started to cry. I touched her face the same way Dakumo touched mine some days earlier. Granny smiled at me and wrapped her hands around me.

The next day, I woke up way before the cock in the compound crowed. I sprang to my feet as soon as my eyelids gave way to the stream of fluorescent light that filled me and Grandma's room. NEPA don bring light. I stood up to reduce the speed of the fan from the control panel. Grandma hated breezy rooms. The clock on the wall showed the time was 4:30 a.m. It is a new day. I went to the bathroom to urinate, came back to the room to check if my bag was properly packed. I tiptoed around the house, trying my best not to disturb Grandma. I took my bath and got dressed in my house clothes. Although my dad was to arrive much later in the afternoon, still, I wasn't ready to take any chances. I wanted to be super ready when he arrived. Grandma was silent all the while as I went about taking my bath, washing the plates in the kitchen. I even attempted to sweep the room with Grandma still sleeping.

"Belema, you know it's not dawn yet. Day never break," she said from under her wrapper as I picked up the broom to sweep.

"But, Granny, I dey try make sure sey everywhere sempe before my paale show face."

"I know you are excited about your father's arrival, but you should take it easy. Day never break, you don baff, wash plate, sweep parlor. You wan even sweep me wey dey sleep join." She sat up on the bed, rubbed her sleepy eyes with the back of her hand. Her wrapper hanged loosely on her chest. Her drooping old-woman breasts in full glare.

I went over to sit with her. I was feeling guilty for being so excited to leave her. I was going to miss her. She took me into her arms and stroked my hair while the bad breath from her unwashed mouth filled my face and my heart. I loved it. I would miss all this. But my father was going to make life heaven for me, I thought.

The Journey

....

My father arrived at noon. He didn't come in a big car like I had imagined. He didn't come with plenty gifts that I could share with my friends. He came empty, just like a rich man who just visited his village during the festive season. He brought with him a small bag filled with gifts for Grandma and three nylon bags of sweet-scented bread loaves. I was on my feet as soon as I heard the horn of a car in the compound. It could only be my father. I just knew. The compound children all ran out when they saw his white Toyota Camry drive into the compound. Shouts of "Uncle Somiari, welcome" filled the air. Children who barely knew him all ran to greet him. Some stretched out on the floor, like they were some respectful bunch. The ones who didn't pretend to be respectful wore bright smiles that tore their ugly faces into beautiful parts. I stood at the door of our room, my flowery-printed gown dancing against the small gust of wind. Seeing all the children run to my dad like he was some government official caused my heart to swell out of proportion with pride. I went to hug him after he gave one of the bread nylons to the children. As I hugged him, he smiled at me and rubbed my head. It felt good.

We were in the house, the package he brought for Grandma sitting idle at the foot of our bedroom. We lived in a room and parlor. As he talked to Granny in their language, the twist of their tongue was too complicated for me to understand. I went to the bag to unravel the things Grandma would be enjoying without me. I was not even halfway across the room when he asked, "Belema, where are you going to?"

His voice was like the steel Papa Ejima, the blacksmith, hammers in his workplace. His voice was mirthless. Innocently, as I've always done with Granny, I answered.

"I want to see what Granny would be enjoying without me." My stride didn't slow a bit as I continued toward the parcel. I bent over and was opening the nylon when I heard Granny's voice. The voice had fear wound around it like Dakumo's wristband.

"Belema, leave that thing and come and sit here. It is wrong to open a person's gift without the person's permission."

"But, Mama, you are not person na. You are my granny," I replied in equal breath, not taking my eye off the milo and cornflakes and the other mede mede provisions in the bag.

"Mama, you will enjoy without me," I continued, unpacking the other things from the gift bag. I didn't even raise my head.

"Would you get yourself out of there before I give you a dirty slap?" a thunderous voice hammered. I stopped unpacking. The voice was steely, thick with anger, like the voice of the devil in the dramas we acted in church.

I got up from there with the speed of a dead snail. I shuffled my feet to the bedroom without saying a word to either Father or Grandma. The world was not falling into pleasant places for me. I heard Granny condemning my father, but I was too pained to listen.

When the images of the toys I would be playing with flooded my head, I quickly forgot about the incident. My happiness returned like it never left. This time, though, there was a caution sign at the entrance of the happiness room. It read: *Be careful*. The former carefree nature of the happiness was snatched away. Now, it strutted around the room looking over its shoulders, looking out for mines and bombs that could trigger the steel voice, or the fiery stare that burnt my skin like hot iron.

I was out of the room faster than I had entered it when Granny called out to me to serve food. The scent of the jollof rice had been disturbing me all morning. The chicken was crisp. Grandma boiled the blended tomatoes and pepper before frying it in oil. When I asked her why she was boiling the blended pepper (since boiling pepper was done for stew and not Jollof), she replied that my father would not eat jollof rice if you didn't boil the pepper. *Pretty strange*, I thought. Who rejects delicious Jollof rice just because you didn't boil the pepper and tomatoes? How would he even know? *This man get problem,* I said to myself.

I understood why my father preferred Jollof rice cooked with boiled pepper and tomato when I tasted the food. That day's jollof was far sweeter than the others Grandma used to cook. I could not wait for my dad to come. I stole some from the pot with the tiny pieces of chicken Grandma usually leaves for me because she knows how much I loved fried meat. She said she leaves tiny pieces of meat for me so that I don't eat the bigger ones whenever I sneaked into the kitchen to steal meat. How she knew I sometimes bit off the large chunks of meat she put in the stew and then refry them before returning the meat to the pot as if nothing happened surprised me.

He wolfed down the mountainous plate of rice Granny served him. I watched as he took each spoon into his mouth. I watched as he grinned while he tore the chicken, the oil dripping from the side of his mouth. Loved how he said "This food sweet o" with his mouth filled with sweet jollof rice. I watched him because he was a spectacle to me. He finished eating, drank a big bottle of Coke before unbuttoning his belt, and relaxing on the couch.

I started eating my rice after he finished. I wanted to impress him, maybe eat like him. I was not even halfway into my food when I took the chicken lap on my plate. I was about tearing the flesh off the bone when Dad shouted, "Wetin you wan do?" The question hit me like a thunderbolt. *What does he mean by what do I want to do? Isn't it obvious? I want to eat my meat. I don't want to kill somebody.*

I dropped the meat back on my plate. Confusion. Surprise. I gave him that what's-wrong-again look.

"You want to eat your meat when you haven't eaten half of your rice?" he asked. His voice was hard as a rock.

"Yes, sir," I muttered, my voice coming out a little lower than I expected. Merely looking at him made me want to hide under a rock.

"You want to eat meat when you have not finished eating your food. Don't you know it's only thieves that behave like that?"

I don't understand what this man is saying. Meat that I have been eating without finishing my food, and Grandma and Grandpa would not say anything. It's the same meat that this man is telling me about thief.

"Is that how your granny has been training you?" He was glaring at me as if he wanted to yank the meat off my hand and thrash me seriously till my butt bled. The image of somebody beating me, or my butt bleeding was terrifying. My grandparents never beat me. I couldn't imagine this man with the soft smile raising his hands to beat me. It was unthinkable.

"No, sir."

"Would you drop that meat back on that plate and finish your rice? Don't you know good children always finish their foods before eating their meat?"

"Why is that?" I asked. My boldness was returning to me.

"Why is what?"

"Why do good children leave their meat until they finish their food before eating it?"

"Because that is what our culture teaches us."

"But Grandma didn't teach me like that. Does she not understand the culture?"

Grandma gave me a cautionary stare. It was that *you-are-going-out-of-line* stare. But there was no stopping me. If this man was my father, he had to learn to deal with me.

Dad looked at me and then he turned to Grandma. The room was as silent as a harmless dream. The space the silence was taking up started to choke me. I wanted to get out of my chair at the corner of the room, flash toward my words, and quickly put them back in my mouth. I knew I had said too much. Although with Grandma, this was not too much. It was a normal conversation. But with this man whom I barely recognized as the man who used to bring me gifts, what I said was very inappropriate.

"You drop your meat and eat that food, else." His final words sealed my fate. I forced the now-gravel-tasting rice down my throat. The food was a metaphor for what I would face in my father's house: pain and gravel.

Point of No Return

....

Going to live with my father was meant to be fun, full of roses, and my dream to live the good city life. Judging from the way he spoke and the gifts he brought for me, I had imagined his house would look like those big mansions I saw in movies. I imagined the compound would be so big that me and my new friends would have excessive space to play and run around. I had also imagined the sitting room to have an aquarium at one corner. In the movies I watched, I loved the houses with aquariums and gardens. I even boasted to a few of my friends that I would bring them bouquets of flowers from my father's garden whenever I visited the village.

But getting to the house, all my lofty images of gardens, a big-sitting room, and a large compound to play in—everything I had imagined my father's house would be—were shattered. I knew my expectations were too high when we had to navigate through pot-holes, smelly gutters, and dirty markets. In the movies, the road to mansions were not smelly, rowdy, and dirty. The roads were properly tiled with well-clad kids, not boys on white singlets cum gray and torn shorts. Not girls and boys with stainless aluminum trays balanced on their heads, or teenagers pushing wheelbarrows loaded with bags of rice, beans, garri, and all manner of goods. What I imagined was far different.

The journey from the village through those bad roads was uneventful. Also atypical of the dad I had imagined. The silence that blanketed us was thicker than the sweater Frank, the boy with two big front teeth, brought when he returned from his holiday in Jos, Plateau State. My dad and I exchanged only ten words.

I said, "Are you happy to have me finally?"

Dad replied, "Yes, I am."

With that, I filled my time counting the number of boys with oranges in trays balanced on their heads. I counted the number of oranges most had on their heads: twenty-two for some, thirty for others. How were they able to balance those trays on their heads and still run so fast without spilling the oranges? For the shirtless boys, their flat chest, just like mine, dripped with brown sweat. I also counted the number of times Dad drove into a pothole, causing us to jerk forward: seven times. I mouthed a "sorry, sir" the first few times, but after his silent response, I kept quiet. He made no effort to buy me gala or Fanta or any snack at all on the road. My throat was parched. I wanted to ask him how much longer it will take to get to the house when he informed me that, as if reading my mind, we would soon be home. We passed a market where women spread their wares on the road close to the gutter. There were children of different ages hawking pure water, oranges, gala, soft drinks, and recharge cards. Flies as big as rats skittered around the gutter. And let's not even talk about the stench of the gutter. The sight gave me flashbacks to when I used to hawk for Grandma. Grandma had a small grocery store, and when her perishable products were almost going bad, she would ask me to hawk them quickly, so she didn't lose money. I enjoyed doing it because she always gave me a tip when I sold out the items on my tray. Unlike the boys who could balance orange trays on their heads, I couldn't. So I always held my tray with both hands. I would hawk at least twice a week when I got back from school and saved my tips to spend in school during lunch break. I hawked at public secondary schools, college of education, polytechnics, and universities. The only thing I dreaded about hawking were the annoying male students who would pretend as though they wanted to make a purchase, but they just wanted to play with my body and try to get me to follow them to their hostel rooms. One time, this man asked me to pack banana and groundnuts for him. I took my time to do the packaging and then I asked for my money. He put his hands in his pocket but brought it out empty. He was acting confused, then he asked me to follow him to his room, which was one block away, to collect my money. I was about to protest when he put his hands around my shoulders to convince me that it wasn't a distance, and he would add a tip for the stress. He looked responsible, so I decided to go with him. I was about to pick up my tray when Aunty Bisi screamed, "Ashewo, leave this small girl and go find your mate!" In less than fifteen minutes, she created a scene, and people gathered. This young man who acted like he lost his money suddenly found money in his wallet to pay me.

It was a trend on campus for young male students to lure naive young female hawkers to their rooms and rape them. Aunty Bisi was in her late twenties. She had been hawking since she was fifteen, and she knew the area very well. She knew about all the mischief and atrocities of the students, and she did her best to protect the children who hawked around the area. Aunty Bisi saved me from getting raped. I didn't tell Grandma what happened that day. I knew she wouldn't let me hawk again if I did, and I didn't want to stop getting my tips. So I kept quiet, but I made sure to always stay around Aunty Bisi every time I went out to hawk.

The sun was already taking a nap beyond the horizon when we turned at a corner where dirty water pooled in the middle of the road. We beelined toward a building painted in brown and blue. An odd color for a building. My heart did a double take. *Is this the house we are going to?* I held back the surprise from displaying on my face. We drove into the building after the main guard, a lanky old man with a broad smile opened the black gate for us.

I got down from the car and was welcomed with stares from children who were better dressed than the ones on the road. There were four children outside the compound with no garden. They didn't say anything. They stood and stared at me as I unloaded my bags from the car's trunk. They greeted my dad and continued talking among themselves.

If the size of the house and its surrounding caused a stir on the sea of my expectations, the woman I saw when I entered the house shifted the shores of that sea to the Sahara. I was shocked beyond words. The shock waves rocked me so hard, I had to support myself by leaning on the wall of the door's entrance.

The woman's neck had ripples of flesh. Her wrapper was tied around breasts that had seen better days but were still trying to hold on for dear life. She didn't look enthusiastic seeing me. She just stood at the door, smiled thinly at me, then she went to collect Dad's bag from him. I dragged my bag into the house. The sitting room was big and gorgeous. There were blue three-seater sofas arranged at opposite angles with two single-seater close to the walls, south of the entrance. To the west of the room, hung on a wall with flower wallpaper as the backdrop, was a thirty-six-inch plasma TV. The parlor smelled nice. I couldn't place a name to the smell. A center table with glass top sat in the middle of the room with a small rug underneath. I figured that the room behind the three-seater couch with a curtain at the entrance was the kitchen. I wanted to sit. I was tired after the three-hour drive, but I knew better than to do that. I stood there, looking around from Father to buxom woman, not knowing what next to do.

"Go to your room, take your bath, and rest," Dad said. This was the first time his voice was level. The woman kept looking at me like I was some antique at the museum. I didn't know where the room Dad talked about was, so I asked him.

"Oh, forgive me. You are new here. That one over there," he pointed to a passageway, dark with a tall humming freezer by the side. "The room to your left, that one with the door closed, is your room. It is quite messy."

I nodded.

"Abi, you don clean am?" he turned to big-bosom woman.

"I no really clean am like that o. But it is clean enough. She has to fold the few clothes on the floor and move them into the wardrobe. It should not take up to ten minutes. Aside that, the room is clean," the woman said. Her gaze never left me. She was studying me.

I dragged my bag to the door. In all my nine years in this world, I had never owned a room of my own. I opened the door, scared and happy at having a room all to myself. The thick scent of washed clothes and detergent smacked against my nose. The room was neat like the woman had said. A few clothes were scattered on the ground: jean trousers, polo shirts, big braziers, and white, black, and red panties. A big mattress, like the one Grandma and I slept on, was on the ground. A purple bedspread, rumpled and unarranged, was on the mattress. A tall wardrobe, so tall I could stand on my head three times but still won't be able to get to the top, hugged the wall. I imagined the person who lived here before had lots of clothes. I was only going to use 0.1 percent of the wardrobe space. My clothes were few.

After I arranged the clothes in the empty wardrobe and kept my bag at one small corner of the wardrobe, I changed into a short and polo shirt. I wanted to take my bath, but I wasn't sure if it was a good idea. I didn't want to ask questions. I didn't want Dad to go all ballistic on me. I hated to see him angry and disappointed.

Taking in the size of the room for a few minutes, I decided to explore. There was a locked door in my room. I figured it led to another room. What was in the other room? I did not know, but I could not help myself. There was no key in the keyhole. I tried the doorknob, squeezed it to the left, hoping it would open. And it did. I pushed the door gently, fear wrapping its big hands around my throat. If this was a forbidden room, then I was as dead as dead. Thinking of what Dad might do to me, I pushed it, nonetheless. That is the problem with me: Fear doesn't stop me from doing whatever I want to do; instead, it fuels my resolve to do it. *"What is the worst that can happen?"* I often ask myself.

The mystery room was the bathroom. The water from the shower rained on me, and it felt so good. The white-tiled walls, the mirror on the wall, and the toilet seat—white and sparkling—made me want to take my bath forever. The room was cleaner than anything I had ever seen. It was not like the nonsense toilet at Granny's place. The whole compound—eight rooms with more than twenty people in total—shared one toilet. This place was heaven.

I was searching my bag for a fresh pair of shorts and a shirt to wear when big-bosom woman bellowed from whichever room she was in. "Belema, won't you come out again? Don't you know you are supposed to come outside to help me cook for your father?"

"I dey come, ma," I replied without thought. I didn't know her name, didn't know who she was. I continued my search. In a bid not to keep her waiting for long, I wore a green polo shirt and the yellow shorts Grandpa bought for me the last time he went to Warri. I dried myself with my towel and hurried to the living room without comb-ing my hair, or rubbing cream on my body.

"This is your aunty, Siyafori. She is my younger sister. She would be helping me take care of you. My work keeps me busy most of the time, so she would be here for you. Ask her whatever you want. She will provide it for you," Dad announced.

I nodded. After father introduced me officially, the not-smiling aunty wore a bright wide smile that covered her beautiful face.

I followed her to the kitchen, and we cooked together. She was not at all bad. Our time together in the kitchen was fun. Not as great as when I cooked with Grandma, but at least she was open to conver-sations, unlike my father who wore a tight lip all the time.

"Your father told me about the rubbish you did today," she started. She was washing the meat in a bowl on the kitchen sink. She squeezed the chunks of beef before dropping them into a pot.

"I didn't do anything o."

"He said you ate your meat before you were halfway into your food."

"Ehn, yes, ma. But what is the big deal? I always do it, and Grandma never complained."

"Your Granny wants to spoil you o. Bele," she said, crunching the cubed spice over the meat. She had added salt and other sachet spices. "When you eat your meat before you finish your food, you—"

"Are a thief?" I interrupted her. "That is what my dad said."

She ignited the gas cooker and placed the pot on it.

"So first, it is rude to interrupt somebody when they are still talking."

"Sorry, ma."

"No problem."

"Second, eating your meat first shows you have no respect for life."

What is this one saying again? I thought. Which one is respect for life? My dad said it was a sign of thieving. Now Aunty Siya is here talking about respect for life. How does meat and life have any connections?

I kept on, watching her, waiting for her lecture. I was used to older people lecturing me.

"When you leave your meat till after you have finished your food, it shows you can be patient, delay gratification, and do the hard work."

"Hard work? Delay gratification? I don't understand, ma." I was rinsing the plates.

"Leaving your meat till after you've finished your food shows that you understand how life works: do the hard job now and enjoy the benefits later. Delayed gratification means you postpone the good thing you can enjoy now for something better in the future."

"So, aunty, what you are saying is that meat is a reward for eating my food?"

"Exactly. It is delaying the reward for later so you can better enjoy it."

"But I enjoy it best when I eat meat when I haven't finished the food."

"Yes, maybe you do, but do you always finish the food after you have eaten the meat?"

"No, ma, I don't."

"That is what I am trying to tell you: You would not finish eating the rice because you have already taken your reward, so there is no motivation."

I kept quiet. Big-bosom woman was making sense. The aroma of the meat—well-spiced meat—wafted from the pot. *She is a good cook*, I reasoned. Not like Grandma, but she knew how to cook.

"Belema, delayed gratification!" she said again, stressing her point.

I had been in the house for two weeks, stuck in the house, when I flunked a rule, disobeyed my aunty. I couldn't go out to play because I was new and knew nobody. Aunty Siya would not even allow me to go outside when the other children were playing in the evening. She said Dad would not be happy with me if I did. But I disobeyed.

Aunty Siya had gone to the market to get foodstuff. I was supposed to follow her, but I feigned a runny stomach. I was purging. She left me at home, warned me not to leave the house until she returned. I said I would not leave. There was noise outside. Children were running and shouting as usual. As soon as she left the gate, I ran out of the house. I went outside to play with the children I didn't know. They were friendly. One of the girls told me she saw me the day I came with my dad, but she hadn't seen me much since then. Another boy with big teeth said he only saw me with my aunty. Was I my father's child? They asked. They were playing police and thief. I was police alongside the girl who saw me the first day I came. Her name was Deborah.

I was too caught up in being police, catching thieves and laughing heartily with Debby and the other children that I did not know when Aunty Siya came back from the market. I didn't know when she entered the house, which I left unlocked, cooked the stew, and had started cooking the white rice. She heard my voice running around, but she decided not to call me. When it dawned on me that she would soon return, I hurried back to the house. I was dazed when I perceived the aroma of stew. She was back. I was in trouble.

"Belema, shebi, I told you not to leave this house till I came back," she said when, in my attempt to tiptoe to my room, she emerged from the kitchen. She was wearing a yellow apron with blue stripes. She was sweating. She cleaned the beads of sweat with the heel of her hand.

"I am sorry, ma," I mumbled. I was truly sorry. But I was happy for the time I spent outside.

"Sorry, abi? Belle no pain you again, abi? I thought you had a running stomach. You left the door opened and went to play police and thief. I came back, met the door open, entered, cooked stew, cooked rice. Still, you didn't show up. If I was a thief now, that's how I would pack everything in the house, and you'd not know. You would be police that can't catch the real thief."

I felt awful. She was right. I should have locked the door.

"Let your father come back. I'll report you to him."

I should have pleaded with her not to, but what could Dad do? I reasoned. I was used to his voice and frequent shouting.

She reported to my dad when he came back from work. He didn't say anything. He looked at me, took his eyes off me while I watched *Tales by Moonlight* on RSTV. I shrunk at his stare.

Two more misbehaviors, and I got the action end of those stares. Dad beat me.

Papa Ejike, our caretaker, had given us bole with stew and fish. He saw us playing outside under the scorching sun. (My aunty now allowed me to play outside since Dad didn't say anything.) Moreover, it gave her time to watch *Super Story* and the other discs she hid under the mattress in her room. We used slippers to make the goalposts. Each person's slippers were placed atop another's, separated a few meters apart. Demola counted the post. At first, he lied to us. He counted five legs for us but counted four and a half legs at his post. It was when his team scored two goals in quick succession that we noticed the flaw in the width of the post Demola had counted. Ours was slightly wider than theirs. And in football games like that, monkey posts, a slight difference in the goal post's width, was a big deal. It could be the reason why one team wins and another loses scandalously. He corrected it when we noticed it. The match ended 4–4.

Papa Ejike saw how swiftly I dribbled Demola, putting the ball in his kolo.

"Yepa! See as girl dey dribble you!" he shouted.

"Belema, sabi play ball o," his wife said.

"You mean am? Is she that good?" he asked, shocked.

"Yes, she is quite good for a girl," Mama Ejike replied.

"If that's the case, when I return, I will buy something for you, kids," he told us. Ejike was on my team. We took his promise lightly. The scores stood at 11–11 when Papa Ejike walked in through the gate with a polybag.

"I brought something for the Messis and Ronaldos."

We stopped playing and ran toward him. He brought out small packages wrapped in black nylon and handed it to us.

"This bole is for you guys. I am impressed by Belema's skill. I never knew a girl could have such skills."

He gave me my package. He gave each of the other five players their own package. We thanked him profusely. He said we were welcome.

As soon as he left, I reached for my nylon, tore it, and was reaching for the content when the other players shouted, "Ehn, what do you want to do?"

"I want to eat my bolly. Which one be stupid question wey una dey ask me?"

"You never show your aunty or your father you wan chop your bole. Nawa for you o," Demola condemned me.

Following their condemnation, I took the bole to Aunty Siya. She was watching Suara and Toyin Tomato on *Super Story*. She told me to keep the bole in her room and wait for my dad to come before eating it.

"But, aunty, I have shown you already. Why can't I eat it?"

"No, you can't. In our culture, you wait for your father or mother to see what a stranger gave you before you eat it."

"Which stupid culture is that one?" I murmured.

"Ehn, what did you say?"

"Aunty, I did not say anything."

"Good. Now go and play. Let me rest."

I was running outside after I had kept the bole in my room when she called out to me, "Belema, don't play too much. We would soon start cooking for your father."

Dad did not return till 9 p.m.

He had just finished eating his pounded yam and Oha soup when Aunty Siya told me to bring the bole.

"Papa Ejike gave Belema bole today," she told him. She gave him the black nylon the bole was wrapped in.

"Okay." He was picking his teeth.

He opened the nylon, peered into it, and dropped it on the table.

"Belema, why did you eat from the bole?"

Aunty Siya's face changed. "Eat from the bole? I told her to keep it and wait for you. She did not—" Dad gave her the nylon.

Meanwhile, I stood there in the parlor, my chest relaxed like a newborn. Nothing will happen. He would only shout.

"Belema, why did you eat from the bole?" Aunty Siya was angry. Her face showed it.

"*Nothing*. I was hungry that's why I ate it."

Tawai! Tawai!

My father's hard palm landed on my face. It deafened my ear temporarily. The music video playing on the television looked like stars running amok in stupid circles. I think they were playing 2Face's "E Be Like Say."

"To my room now!" he barked. I shuffled my feet to his room. How I moved my feet, I don't know, but I found myself moving.

Inside his room, my ear was ringing. The slap felt like somebody took a big lump of wood and drove it into my ear, blocking every sound. Then the big wood, already inside my ear, started to beat itself, like a local drum. I was partially deaf and hearing strange music. Later, still waiting for him to come inside, the wood started hitting places in my head I couldn't recognize. My head started to ache badly.

He came in three minutes later. I knew because I was unconsciously counting the tick of the black clock on the wall of his room.

"Why do you want to spoil yourself like this, ehn, Belema?"

I was lost. I was spoiling myself. How? All I did was cut from the bole—it was small I cut sef—before wrapping it with the foil as if nothing happened. I didn't even take much from the fish.

He removed his belt. Stretched it. I started to move toward the bed. My heart was sinking in slow motion. The burp of water filled my ear. I was dead. I have never been beaten. His eyes turned to the back of his head, and another eye I could never have imagined replaced his old eyes. He locked the door behind him. I wanted to explain, to tell him I was sorry and would never do it again. But I found the stone in my throat too heavy to swallow. I opened my mouth. Air seeped out; words couldn't.

He grabbed me on my left hand. His grip was firm, like a tourniquet around an arm of a sick patient. He dragged me from the corner I was hiding. He raised his belt to hit me. I raised my free hand to block the belt from touching me. The belt struck my thumb. I felt my bone shift. I screamed so loud I thought I would tear my voice box. He pushed me to the bed and started to beat me all over my body. The belt fell on my face, on my head, on my stomach. Every part of my body received the pelting. I turned from one side to the next, trying to avoid the belt.

As I turned, he followed me rhythmically, each strike hitting me in new places. The pain rippled through me like flashes of current. I yelped as he flogged me. He didn't stop. My skin was burning with each pelting. After about ten minutes—it felt like an hour though— each strike of the belt started to peel my skin. He had struck every free space on my body. The violet marks were ripe for bursting. As he kept beating me, the stinging pain started to give way to numbness. I felt my skin break at the back of my neck. Blood. I tasted the blood in my subconscious before I saw it. It dribbled into my mouth. Blood. My mind started to lose grasp of reality. He kept beating me with increased velocity. The higher he raised his hands to hit me, the harder the belt struck. The more he beat me, the faster he got. His biceps were getting used to the exercise.

I kept screaming, hoping Aunty Siya would knock on the door. I was hoping that she would beg him to stop flogging me the same way people used to do at Granny's compound. Nothing. Not even a knock on the door. He kept beating me till I lost my voice. I couldn't scream again. I opened my mouth to scream, but nothing came out. It was a hoarse cry, like an animal breathing his last. He didn't stop, didn't reduce his intensity. He was an enraged beast, and I couldn't explain why. I only ate from the bole (that was given to me). I was stretched on the floor of my father's room, unmoving. I allowed him to beat me as he wished.

My body was dead. My unconscious and subconscious minds started a conversation.

Mind one asked, "Is it more than the bole I ate?"

Mind two replied, "No o. I wonder why he is so angry."

Mind one said, "Something annoyed him at work today."

Mind two asked, "So what? What could annoy a man that he wants to kill his daughter?"

Mind one asked, "Does this have anything to do with his past with my mother?

Mind two replied, "Maybe. Remember when you asked him about her, he just said you were a mistake that should never have happened?"

Mind one asked, "Are you not already dead?"

Mind two replied, "I don't think so. I can still see him beating my body."

Mind one said, "He said he could kill you if he wishes. He is your father."

Mind two asked, "Is that what he said? When did he say it?"

Mind one said, "You are not even listening to him. He said it some moments ago."

Mind two asked, "How many minutes, specifically?"

Mind one replied, "I no know o. You still dey calculate specificity for this kain situation."

Mind two asked, "Wetin you want make I do na?"

Mind one asked, "Won't you die already?"

Mind two asked, "Why are you giving me the task of dying? Can't you do the dying?"

Mind one replied, "I am not ready yet."

Mind two said, "Neither am I."

Darkness.

The last voice I heard was Aunty Siya's. She was telling Dad to stop. My blurry vision saw her standing at the entrance of Dad's room, her full-body frame filling the door's frame. He stopped beating me. I heard him drag his feet toward the door, opened the door, and somebody rushed toward me.

Then as the darkness began to close in on me, I heard Aunty Siya say, "She's not breathing again. Ahn Ahn bros, see as blood full her body. You wan kill her?" The darkness closed in on me, and everything turned black.

Father of Nightmares

....

Living with my father and Aunty Siya started to feel like a weird dream, one I desperately wanted to awaken from but was unable to. There were happy days. There were days when the light in my dad's eyes lit like neon lights. There were days when he took us out to get ice cream and donuts, days when he bought me toys and all those things he used to buy for me when I was living with Grandma. But those days were far and few between. I was so scared of him. I started to ask fewer questions. I hadn't noticed it until one day when I talked to Grandma. She had called Aunty Siya to speak to me.

See ehn, no matter how not so conducive the house was for me, I couldn't complain to Granny. Dad beat me very often, so I knew I had to be cautious around him. And Aunty Siya too.

"Belema, this one you are answering me yes and no. What is the problem?" It was a Saturday afternoon. We had akara and ogi for breakfast. Dad was out to watch football with his friends. Aunty Siya was paging through a fashion magazine. There was no light, so the house was stuffy. I wore a white singlet and brown shorts.

"Granny, nothing is wrong. I am fine. I am just tired."

"Which kind of tired would make you not ask me questions and ask after your friend, Dakumo?"

"Oh, how is she doing?" I asked absentmindedly. I had missed her badly. I often thought of her whenever I felt alone. Here I had Debby, but she wasn't as understanding as Dakumo. Moreover, Debby didn't have breasts. Dakumo had breasts, and I was also looking forward to having breasts.

"She is fine. She has been asking me when you would be coming with the toys you promised her. She can't wait."

"Tell her very soon." I wanted to tell Granny to tell her that there were very few toys here. That I'll give up living here to come back to the village to live with her and Granny and Suor and to use the dirty toilet and listen to Granny's sometimes-boring nuggets. I wanted Granny to help me tell her here wasn't as fun as I had expected. But I shut my mouth and answered Granny's question as enthusiastically as I could. The call lasted two minutes, thirty seconds. Silence filled one minute of those two minutes. Granny couldn't understand why I was the way I was, and I, too, didn't know why I was that way. Silence was the best form of communication in this house.

But my quiet didn't last long. News of me starting school got my caged bird excited. It fluttered its wings and sang in its sweet voice. I danced and danced the day Dad announced I would be starting school the next week. The house was beginning to make a desert of my happiness. Maybe leaving the house would bring me some raindrops and brighten my gray.

Aunty Siya took me to the school. All I had to do was fill out a form, while Aunty Siya went back to the house. The guy who asked me questions as he typed the answers into the computer was tall and fair-skinned with an oval-shaped face. He had three scars on his left arm, two long fingernails on his right hand, and two tribal marks on his face—one on both sides. His teeth were white, except for a brown stain on the fifth molar to the left. He typed quite fast. I was envious.

I was taken to my class, JSS1. The class was the third class in a row of classes. Once we got to the entrance of the class, the registration guy told me to walk in. "Shouldn't you introduce me to the students first?" I asked him. I was tense. My blue jean trousers and white shirt would make me stand out from the rest of the uniform-wearing students. I should at least get an introduction. I can't do this alone.

The registration guy told me to enter the class, and I'll be welcomed. The noise coming from the class was piercing, gritty on the ears like a whooping swarm of bees. Tiny voices from children I was sure would not like me floated incessantly from the class. I heard "*Idiots! Fool!*" from female voices.

Seeing my trepidation, registration guy with three scars on his left arm and a brown stain on his teeth decided to enter the class with me.

"*Good* morning, sir," the class chorused.

"Good morning, guys," registration guy responded.

"I have with me here a new student. Her name is—" He turned to me. That was my cue to say my name.

"Belema," I replied, forcing a smile. The class wasn't impressed.

Then one guy at the back, in the fourth row, started laughing.

"Why are you laughing, Emeka?" registration guy asked. I was still standing with him.

"What kind of name is Belema? Is that even English?"

"Emeka, shut up and stop laughing," registration guy bellowed. "Belema, go to the back. Sit with Shina." He pointed toward an empty seat with a dark-skinned girl with small rabbit-like ears and full lips seated on one part of the chair. There were twenty-two students in the class—thirteen girls and nine boys. I would make the number twenty-three. I walked up to Shina, beamed at her, removed my bag from my back, and sat down.

"Shina, make sure you take care of her. She is new, and as the class captain, you need to see to it that she feels comfortable." With that said, the registration guy left the class. That was how Shina and I became friends.

But I was only close to Shina. The other students always laughed at me because of how I spoke. Before that time, I didn't know I had an accent. My words were as normal as everybody I knew. There was no need to hide my tongue in the cave of silence. There was no need to answer in monosyllabic words, ashamed of how funny I sounded. Whenever I pronounced a word wrongly, which was most times, they would call me Bele the Cele. I didn't know what cele meant, but I knew it was an insulting word. My words didn't slur, but whenever they mimicked me, they sounded like the words were being dragged out of their mouth by a tractor. I cringed inside anytime they did this. I would feign a laugh, but deep down, I was dying. I wanted to take my revenge out on them.

And I found a perfect time for it.

Shina informed me some days before that she wouldn't be coming to school on Tuesday. She was traveling to the village with her parents to bury her grandmother. It was sad to think of Granny dying. I won't be able to stand it. On Monday, our mathematics teacher announced to the class that we would have a mathematics test the next day. Math was in the morning, first period.

I woke early, did my house chores, and was ready to go to school by 7 a.m. Aunty Siya was surprised at my early preparation, knowing how she usually forced me to be fast with my bathing and eating in the morning. She got a call from a friend while she was preparing to take me to school. It was an emergency.

"Can you go to school yourself?" she asked me as she applied her makeup. She always wore makeup whenever she was going out, even if it was down the road to buy pure water.

"I can, aunty," I replied, trying to hide my excitement.

"Hen! This one you are ready so early. Hope it isn't one boy that has been deceiving you that's making your body do gbiri gbiri so."

I didn't respond. Small talk with Aunty Siya was good and bad. She could easily report me to Dad, and I wasn't ready to face any of his madness. Yes, there was a boy who liked me. Maybe it was my head thinking he liked me o, but this boy in JSS3, Sochima, was always looking at me during break, smiling like a sheep. He hasn't talked to me yet, but Shina thinks he is into me. I can't tell Aunty Siya that kind of thing na, you know. She might tell Dad, and hell will break loose on my body. Never. I was not ready for more beating.

I was the first in my class to come to school. I was the tenth person in the whole school that day. Registration guy, Moses, hadn't come yet. The bursar was around. She lives very close to the school. Sometimes I wonder if she slept in the school. I went straight to my class to inspect if any other person had come. Nobody. Each student had a locker where they kept their books and stationeries. Many of us left the locker opened because what could a person steal. There was nothing of value in the locker. Well, they didn't know there was something of immense value, but they had been overlooking it all the while. I opened each student's locker, took all their erasers and pencils, and went outside to play.

"You all should get ready for your mathematics test this morning," the lanky mathematics teacher announced. *He was looking handsome today*, I thought. His pink shirt and black trousers looked silk, and those black pointy shoes he wore was polished to the sheen. They were glowing like the bald head of Mr. Pariolodo, our principal.

"I don't want any excuses. Nobody should tell me they haven't read. I told you about this test one week ago." He stepped out of the class so we would get the paper, pens, and pencils we needed for the test.

As soon as he left, everybody started opening their lockers, taking out their notebooks, turning to the middle to see if there were free pages to tear off for the test. I did the same.

Then just like a musical concert, the complaints started floating. It was Praise that first raised the alarm of his missing "biro." Then Stella. Followed by Francis. Soon, the whole class was murmuring about their pens.

I joined the complainers.

"I can't find my pen. Who took my pen?" Tamuo complained.

"There is a thief in this class, o, hey!" Stella shouted. That Warri girl. She was always too loud and always too forward. Idiot.

Mr. Mathematics Teacher entered the class room three minutes later to meet the bedlam.

"What is happening here?" he inquired.

"We can't find our writing materials," I replied. I wanted to be vocal so that everyone knew I wanted us to find the thief in our class. "Who dare comes into our class and steals our biros?"

He was confused. He looked at the disconcerted class, listened to the murmurings and accusations and counteraccusations about who stole the pens. He sighed.

"Guys, don't worry. I have a solution to this problem."

And the solution saw me opening my bag after fifteen other classmates had opened theirs. I was terrified as I unzipped my bag and shut my eyes. The whole class stood behind him, everybody eager to know who stole the pens so they would call the person a thief. I knew this was going to be nasty. Mr. Mathematics Teacher searched my bag, pouring out all its contents. Spilled from the bag were notebooks, nylon wrappers of chewing gum and biscuits, and small pieces of paper where I wrote imaginary letters to my imaginary boyfriend. Nobody bothered reading the notes on the paper. It was a normal thing to find scraps of paper in a student's bag.

"There is nothing in her bag," Mr. Mathematics Teacher announced. The exercise continued. He searched the other students. He found nothing.

Having spent more than half of his forty-minute period (It was not half. He spent twenty-eight minutes and fifty seconds searching for the missing pen.), he decided, in his magnanimous wisdom, to buy a new pen for all of us. We wrote the test and were happy. It was a simple test.

We were in our last period when a senior from SS2 came to our class to tell me the principal wanted to see me.

"For what?" I asked him.

"I don't know. He only asked me to call Belema in JSS1."

"Okay, thank you."

There was no teacher in class, so I packed my books inside my bag as everyone else did the same. Seeing what happened that day, nobody wanted to risk their books and "biros" again. It was better to suffer the burden of the books on your shoulders than lose them.

I entered the principal's office to meet a bunch of "biros" on his table. He glowered at me. I sat down without his permission.

"You know how these pens got here, don't you?" His voice was hoarse and drenched in anger.

I nodded.

"You know the implication of what you did, right?"

I nodded.

"Are you going to explain why you did it, or do you want to continue nodding like an agama lizard?"

I shook my head in the negative.

"Very well, then, I will report your case to the disciplinary committee. But before that, I have called your father. He said he would handle this himself. Still, I'll hand you over first to the school's counselor. When she finishes with you, the disciplinary committee will deal with you. Is that understood?"

I did not nod. I stared at the blank space on the wall not covered with wallpaper. I also noticed a tiny spot on his bald head with tiny strands of hair sprouting like a plant in the Sahara.

"Belema, can you hear me?"

No response.

My classmates are the cause of their misfortune. They made me do this.

The gray hair strands were around five or so tiny things. Tears started to stream down my cheeks as I stared at the space on the wall.

"Oh, you want to cry your way out of this, ehn? No way," he said as spittle flew out of his mouth and dropped on my left arm. It stank like a pit latrine.

He stank, like the other stupid students. He stank. He, his school, and the idiotic counselor who told me to take care of things when I reported to her that my classmates were insulting and bullying me. They all stank. And the idiot thought I wanted to escape the school's punishment. Fool. Big bald fool! He didn't even know what awaited me at home.

Stupid principal! You shouldn't have called my father! You should have kept the whole matter shush, shush as a good principal should. But, no, you carried your leprous hands to call him, to tell him I stole my classmates' pen and hid it in the toilet. You fool, you called him that a student in SS2 saw me when I hid it behind the toilet seat, and the stupid student reported me. Why did the idiot talk? Dear stupid principal, I wrote in my mind, *I am not crying because I want to escape whatever silly punishment you and your stupid staff will mete out to me. I am crying because of what my father will do to me. And that, dear bald-headed principal, is far worse than what you and your minions could ever do.*

When I got home, I was scared as hell of what awaited me when my father returned. I walked around the house with fear wrapped around my throat. I did not speak too many words. I was saving my strength for the beating. Dad arrived two hours earlier than his usual time. He drove into the compound around 5:00 p.m. I was in my room, trying to do my social studies assignment. There was power. Voices from the actors on African Magic seeped into my room. Dinner was ready, so Aunty Siya and I could do whatever we liked.

I tried all I could to avoid my dad, but there was no avoiding him. I served him his dinner in silence, trying my best to avoid eye contact. He called me to the living room.

I shuffled my feet as I walked to the living room, fear and trepidation clawing their way into my soul. I stood before him with sweat dripping under my armpit. There was power. The television's audio was muted. A football match was on. I think it was an old match.

"Go on your knees," he barked.

"Yes, sir."

I went down without complaint.

My insides tingled like a billion bullet ants were stinging me. I wished the ground would open for me to fall into. My palms became sweaty. I clasped my hands, closed my eyes, and prayed to God that Dad would not beat me. I wanted to tell him that I was sorry, that I didn't mean to do it, and that I just wanted revenge on my classmates for all the insults and bullying. But I swallowed the words.

He looked at me with so much contempt, I felt like a piece of useless furniture. He crossed his feet, kept his gaze on me, and shook his head. I knew that head shake. It was the shake of a man who had given up on his child. I imagined he thought I was a disgrace, a mistake he should never have accepted. In that moment, kneeling before my father, I wished my mother had not left me. I wished she were here to plead my case. Or maybe if I was with her, I wouldn't be going through this torture. I wished my mother existed.

"Crawl to that pillar," he ordered with a cold steely voice. He pointed to the pillar at the dining area entryway. The pillar had a picture of a tree wrapped around it.

I slowly crawled to the pillar.

"Hug the pillar."

I hugged it.

He went into his room. When he came out a few seconds later, he held a rope. I was still hugging the pillar and praying silently that he would change his mind. He did not. He wound the rope around my body. He tied me to the pillar. Aunty Siya was nowhere in sight.

"Why did you steal the biros?" he asked. He wasn't asking. He was telling me. There was no question mark after biros. He wanted to know what possessed me to steal pens. It was a full stop. Just a big empty full stop. Nothing else.

I didn't respond to the question statement.

Koboko, a whip made from dried cow skin, usually the tail, surfaced from nowhere.

"I am going to teach you a lesson you would never forget in a long time. Stealing from your classmates is a no-no in my house. Do you understand?"

"Yes, sir."

He struck me with the koboko. The pain was sharp. It stung in ways I never expected. My back burnt with so much intensity I tried to break free from the rope to massage my wound a little.

I suppressed the yelp, swallowed the pain with the cry.

But I couldn't. Dad kept on striking me with the koboko, tearing my flesh faster than the whip did the last time. I screamed, begged, yowled, and tried to thrash my bounded hands and legs. Being stuck to a pillar and getting flogged is the worst kind of punishment one could ever experience.

After twenty minutes of pelting me so hard that I lost my voice from screaming and begging, he untied me. I was starting to slip into darkness, just like the last time. That day, however, my two minds were not chattering. They kept silent. I was bathed in blood, and red stripes and pain took me by the hand and was leading me down its home. Dad asked me to strip, I took off everything I was wearing, and then, like a sheep being led to the slaughterhouse, he ordered me to go outside. It was then Aunty Siya tried to plead with him.

"Bros," she said, holding his hands, "this one wey you wan do no follow na. E too much. You don beat this girl reach." Her eyes were misty. She was crying for me.

He gave her the meanest stare I had ever seen. She knew better than to continue begging. He yanked his hands off, grabbed me on my right arm, and dragged me outside. I was too weak to protest, too broken to feel ashamed. It was evening. People were returning from work.

My father dragged me through the streets of Rainbow Estate, naked, red koboko marks on my skin, and bloodstains all over me. He didn't say anything. He just dragged my near-lifeless body around. People stared at him—boys, girls, men, women. They all looked at us like a spectacle, but none stopped him. Nobody asked him why he was dragging a naked girl around the street. Nobody questioned him for the blood on my body, or the koboko marks. Nobody did anything. Nobody said anything. Nobody. I was dead meat. No need asking questions over dead meat.

Old Wine Ages Well

....

If life were a bed of roses, I am sure Dad would have shouted the roses into thorns. He had a penchant for flaring up at the slightest provocations. Something was always gnawing at him, slowly chipping away at his happiness. Then one morning, he woke with the brightest of smiles and deepest laughter we had experienced. Aunty Siya was skeptical about his new happiness, and she told me. It was a Saturday. We were making our Saturday special, akara. Aunty Siya was mixing the semiliquid bean flour while I sliced onions and pepper.

"This one my dad is happy like this. Wetin happen?" Aunty Siya and I had become closer after Dad's embarrassing beating and street parade. She sympathized with me. It was her who treated me well that week when I didn't go to school.

"I don't know o, but I suspect it is a woman."

"A woman. How do you mean?" I was on the last seed of pepper.

"So you don't know your father has been seeing a woman all these while?"

I knew, or to be more specific, I noticed, but I was too afraid to prod any further, or ask him if he was seeing anybody. The consequences of my asking were dire.

"I noticed he was always smiling whenever he was on the phone. But recently, he just became an embassy for moodiness."

"Yes. I suspect he fought with the woman. Maybe they've reconciled." She collected the plate of sliced pepper and onions, poured it into the semiliquid bean flour, and continued mixing. She added a few pinches of salt.

49

"Hmm, what does this mean? Would he take us to buy ice cream today?" I asked, half expecting her to laugh and then tell me it would not happen today. Ice cream on Dad's happy days was me and Aunty Siya's side joke.

"Ice cream? Is that what you are thinking about? You don't know what is going on o, this girl."

I was confused.

I rinsed the last of three plates I was washing. Aunty Siya hated dirty plates in the sink whenever she was cooking.

"What do you mean I don't know what is going on?"

"Don't you know if your father and this woman reconcile, she might come live with you and your father?"

"Come live with us as what?"

"As your father's wife, of course."

"Where would you go? Why didn't you say, 'She would come live with us'?"

"Belema, you dey make me laugh. The main reason I am here is so I can help your dad take care of you. As soon as another woman comes, I am out of this house."

The information hit me hard. Aunty Siya wasn't the friendliest of persons, but recently, we have been talking a lot more. If she leaves, it will take a toll on me. She sensed my unease.

"Don't worry. I'm sure the woman would be nice and understanding." She forced a smile. It was so bogus.

One thing about Aunty and my dad is that they didn't think I had feelings. They didn't think things affected me emotionally. Aunty didn't bother asking me how I felt about Dad's supposed wife. Dad didn't think it was necessary to ask for my opinion on him getting a wife. Not like I had a say in what he did with his life, but at least, I was supposed to be an important part of it.

Dad announced, while we were having breakfast, that we would be going for dinner in the evening. He wanted us to meet somebody special. Nobody was happy. We knew who this special person was, and we were not particularly interested in seeing a woman who might undo the fabric of our small family. A fabric I was beginning to get used to.

"We leave by 5 p.m.," he said casually, munching on his akara before taking a spoonful of ogi.

I couldn't wait for evening. As the day crawled by like a lazy snail, I pictured what it would look like having another woman in the house. Since Aunty Siya told me about the possibility of Dad getting married, I had mixed feelings. I had not met my biological mother, but something in me still felt unsafe with another woman. Not like I really had a say with whom my father decided to spend the rest of his life with, but I felt another woman would be an invasion, an intrusion I wasn't ready for.

I also imagined, in my young innocent mind, what the woman would look like. Would she be as beautiful as the women I saw on television and my teachers at school? Would she be like those wicked stepmothers in the movies? What would be her favorite soup? Would she even like me? The thought of her not liking me scared me. I asked Aunty Siya what she thought of this "special person" we were going to meet at dinner, and all she said was "Let us see what happens. I don't know the person. All we can do is wait."

"But, aunty o, why does Daddy need another woman?" I asked her while she tapped incessantly on her Android phone.

"What kind of question is that one again? Your dad is a man and he needs a woman in his life."

"But you are here."

"It is different," she replied, eyes still focused on her phone. She laughed and continued typing. I think she was chatting on WhatsApp.

"Erm, aunty o, is that why Dad has been acting a bit nice the last few days?" I asked.

"Aha! You also noticed it. I thought I was the only one who noticed the sudden change o." The light on her phone's screen went dim. She dropped the phone on the sofa and faced me. Now she was giving me her attention.

"It is not only you o, aunty. I have also noticed the perfume he has been wearing. They are different."

"Yes! Yes!" Aunty Siyaofori exclaimed. "The perfume is very—" She laughed at the thought. She didn't complete her statement.

51

"And did you also notice he comes back late from work and still says he is not hungry?"

"Of course, na," Aunty Siya said. "When a man has eaten food that made his tongue sing hallelujah from another woman, the one in his house would bore him." Her phone beeped. A WhatsApp message.

"I don't understand, Aunty Siya."

"What I am saying is that since your dad found a person's food that was more delicious than what we cook at home, he had to stop eating at home. Our food no dey sweet again," she replied. Aunty Siya always found a way to make jokes of serious matters.

Well, for me, I didn't mind him not eating our food. What I was most concerned about was how this new woman would affect me and my dicey relationship with my father. I only had to wait a few more hours before I knew what dark clouds were moving into my future.

The restaurant was the fanciest I have ever been to. There were beautiful drawings of trees and a lion and a tiger protecting its young one. To the far-left corner of the restaurant, a DJ was playing soft jazz music. I couldn't recognize the artist playing, but the guitar progression blended perfectly with the keyboard. We walked to a table, Dad in front, Aunty Siya behind him, while I trailed her. We settled on a table at the far-left side of the restaurant. The air conditioner was in full blast. I wish I had worn something thicker.

"She should be here any moment now," Dad said, leafing through the menu.

"What do you want, Bele?"

"Anything will do."

"Go through the menu and choose something for yourself. Today is a special day. I have a special announcement to make."

I eyed aunty. She winked.

"Siyaofori, what do you want?"

"Let me see what they have."

Aunty Siya ordered spaghetti and plantain. Dad ordered fried rice, and I ordered jollof rice, fried rice with plantain. The waiter was leaving when a lady, tall with dimples, walked toward our table. From the way she was smiling, I could tell she was the one Dad wanted us to meet. I held my breath. This was going to be some dinner.

Dad stood to hug her. He pecked her on both cheeks. She smelled good. I liked her perfume.

"Guys, meet my woman, Damaris."

My woman! Dad used my woman for somebody. Popsy was in love.

I got out of my chair to greet her.

"Good evening, ma'am."

"Good evening, Belema." She was nice. I also liked her smile.

Aunty Siya said Hi and Beautiful Damaris sat down.

"What do you want?" Dad asked her in a singsong voice I had never heard before. The glint in his eyes could blind anyone who looked at them for too long. My father was clearly in love.

The DJ switched to Celine Dion's "My Heart Will Go On," the theme from *Titanic*. The music was perfect for the occasion. Dad was in love, and I was about to have a stepmother. I was uncertain about my future with this new combination.

Midway into the meal, Dad said he wanted to make a toast. He poured red wine for Aunty Siya and his girlfriend and poured a Fanta for me. We clinked our glasses. He toasted to life, to love, to prosperity, and a happy home. He hadn't told us anything yet. We were waiting.

When he finished the toast, he settled into his chair, sipped from his wine, and looked at Aunty Siya and me.

"I want to tell you ladies that I will be getting married to Damaris. We have been in love for a while. We have been seeing each other for almost a year. The last weeks have been hard for me. You all must have noticed my temper and moodiness, thicker than London fogs. It was her fault." He touched her lightly on her shoulder.

"I asked her to marry me, but she said she wasn't sure." He was talking so fast, as if he wanted to get the words out of his mouth, out of his head before they decayed. It was as if he had been rehearsing the lines he would say for a long time. "Last night," he continued, his gaze fixed on me, trying to tell me something I couldn't understand, "she agreed to marry me. She finally decided to spend the rest of her life with me, and I am super excited about it."

He allowed a few seconds to pass before continuing.

"I know I should have told you ladies before now, but I didn't know how to put it. It is my responsibility to inform you guys on a decision as important as this, and I am sorry."

He might not have told us, but he had acted all too friendly for us not to notice. We just didn't want to tell him we saw the brighter smile he wore. And the perfumes that filled the house in the mornings. Or the late nights he spent on his phone laughing away and sending voice notes. We saw the signs, Aunty Siya and I.

Damaris frowned at his statement. She shifted in her chair. I saw her cast a hot stare at my dad before masking it with a bogus smile. She didn't approve of him apologizing.

The months leading to her arrival in our house was a tough one for me. Coming to terms with the incoming wife wasn't easy for me. Knowing that I would soon have a stepmother caused me sleepless nights. A week after the dinner, I started having nightmares where I saw Damaris trying to chop off my hand with a sharp glistening machete.

When I first told Aunty Siya about my dreams, she laughed at me and told me to stop overthinking. She assured me, in that Aunty Siya way, that nothing like that would ever happen. I didn't believe her. The next day, I narrated the dream to my father when he returned from work. He was focused on his phone and laughing those kind of Aunty Siya laughs that came in short bursts. He was obviously chatting with his wife-to-be. Dad was incredibly happy that night. He listened quietly as I spoke. He also told me, just like Aunty Siya, that I was seeing things because I was scared. He assured me that Damaris was a good woman. He said she would love me as if I were her own daughter.

"Nothing will happen to you. Damaris is too caring a woman to hurt you. She can't even hurt a fly," my father boasted. He hugged me that night before sending me off to my room. That was the first time my father hugged me since I started living with him. Damaris was having a positive effect on him.

Three days later, I had a similar dream. This time, however, she was not chopping off my hand. In the dream, I was walking home when I saw her and three hefty men. I did not greet them. I walked past them as if they were ghosts. She called me back and ordered me to greet her. I refused, insisting she was not my mother and, therefore, had no right to demand any form of greeting from me. She then ordered the men to deal with me.

The men bounded me and took me to an uncompleted building, tied my hands and feet, and started beating me with their belts. They had beaten me until I could feel blood on my tongue. Then seeing I was losing strength, one of them pulled down his brown trousers, revealing an erect mound of flesh, jutting behind his boxer shorts. He gave me a wry smile, and I knew what was coming. The fear of getting raped made me cry out in a piercing voice out of the dream. I woke sweating profusely like a Christmas goat. I managed to stay awake that night until the next morning. And as soon as Dad left for work about 6 a.m., I hurried to Aunty Siya's room. I begged her to call Grandma for me.

"Why do you want to talk to your grandmother this early?" she asked when I requested the call.

"I remembered something that I want to tell her. I don't want it to leave my head," I lied. I could not tell her it was a dream again. I feared she might laugh at me like she did the first time. She called Grandma for me after looking at me funny. She suspected something was wrong. But she didn't say.

Grandma's voice boomed with excitement when she heard my voice. I went to my room so that Aunty Siya wouldn't overhear me and Mama's conversation. I told Mama about the dream, narrating how the men even tried raping me before I screamed out of the dream.

"My child, no evil shall near you," she prayed. "Nothing anybody does will have any effect on you. The blood of Jesus would guide and protect you," she continued. I could picture Mama shutting her eyes, walking around the sitting room while praying for me. She might even snap her fingers as the prayer got hotter. She probably even bumped into a sofa. I kept answering "amen" to all her prayers, which, to be honest, felt like eternity. I needed that assurance, no matter how long it took. I needed somebody to listen to me and take me seriously. I wished I had a mother.

They didn't get married in the church because Dad rarely went to church. She came in one day with her boxes of clothes, a blank face, and many troubles. Aunty Siya left a day before Damaris's arrival. The atmosphere in the house, after Aunty Damaris moved in, wore a metallic feel. Her presence and demeanor were heavy. It became stricter and, to be honest, cleaner. She was a great cook, I'll give her that, but she rarely cracked a smile. I wore my cloak of silence like my Christmas cloth, my finest clothes. Silence became my favorite attire.

There was no need for Aunty Damaris to shout at me or beat me, but she looked for the slightest opportunity to spank me. She would give me house chores that kept me busy from the time I returned from school until night when my father would return from work. I was working my butt off, spending less time with my friends, and sliding into depression.

One day, after I returned from school, bent over washing the mountain of clothes she packed for me, she brought her panties for me to wash. I didn't mind doing anything for her so long as I had my peace of mind. But when she dropped the panties on the ground for me, I saw they were panties I washed yesterday. "Aunty Damaris," I called, "I washed these panties yesterday."

"I know, but they aren't as clean as I want them to."

My head rang. Wasn't as clean? Are you kidding me?

We had a washing machine, but she would rather I washed her clothes with my hands. She said washing machines were bad for some fabrics. Hand washing was better. I told Dad about it, but he shrugged, told me I should obey my stepmother, and stop complaining.

"Aunty, it is unfair for me to wash these panties after I washed them yesterday. If they aren't as clean as you want it, you can use the washing machine. I am tired of washing these panties every time." I was tired of the nonsense. *If I perish, I perish*, I reasoned.

"Are you talking to me like that?" she asked, surprised I could speak more than three words at a time.

"Aunty, I am tired. I have homework waiting for me, books to read for our test tomorrow. I am tired. Please," I continued. I knew I could not continue with my stubbornness. It would only earn me more knocks on the head and slaps, insults, and chores. "Aunty, can I wash them tomorrow? I promise I'll wash them as soon as I return from school."

She stood still for a minute, thought of it, and dropped the panties on my head.

"If you know what's good for you, don't wash these panties." She stormed off.

Her treatment was making me lose weight. Dad was not concerned. The more I tried to please her, the more I failed. I resigned after a while to do whatever I wanted. Not like I was going to disrespect her, I decided not to try too hard to please her anymore.

My decision to live my life the best way I could by dumping every good-girl behavior didn't earn me credit. Instead, I got harsher treatment. She gave me food without meat, allowed me to stay hungry for hours before dishing a small portion on a plate for me. Money for snacks wasn't given me, and I didn't complain.

But one day, Aunty Damaris made me so angry, I decided to do something to pay her back. There was nothing I could do to her directly, so I opted for something else: stealing. I learned extremely fast that whenever I misbehaved, she got enraged. Why was she enraged? I don't know, but it got her blood boiling, as well as that of my dad's. So when she made me angry that day, I decided to touch her anger button. I decided to steal Shina's snacks money.

Shina usually brought one hundred naira to school to buy snacks. Most times, she would give me from her biscuit and sausage roll. Shina and I were best friends, so it was unreasonable of me to steal from her. But I had to. I needed to let off the burning anger inside me. Shina keeps her money in her socks, making it impossible for somebody to steal.

We were having mathematics when I stole the money from her socks. Engrossed in the simultaneous equation the teacher was teaching, I bent under our desk, pretending to pick up my pen. I deftly rolled her socks and removed the money from her leg. She was so caught up in the teaching that she did not notice. When it was time for break, she bent to remove her money but saw nothing. She was hysterical. She started crying. She hadn't eaten at home that day, she said. The money was for her breakfast and dinner. She also said she was going to report it to the principal.

"But you usually kept your money in your socks. How did it get missing?" Gineka asked.

"How would I know? I will go and report all of you o."

"Are you sure you brought the money to class?" another boy asked her. We had investigators in our class.

"I am very sure. I kept it in my socks when I was at home. The money is new."

I wanted to tell her the money was with me, but I was too afraid to tell her. Seeing the pain in her eyes, I realized Aunty Damaris hurting me was not a good enough reason to hurt my best friend. The mini investigation was going on when I slipped out of the class to ease myself. I hurried to the food vendor, bought rice for thirty naira, meat for thirty-five naira, and one sachet of pure water. I brought it to the class and gave it to Shina.

"Since you did not eat this morning, take this," I stretched the plate toward her.

She was unsure of my gesture.

"Where did you get money from, Belema?" she asked, suspicious.

"Something happened. I'll tell you later. Just eat."

She collected the food from me and wolfed down the rice. I gave her the thirty-five change during lesson time.

"Where did you see money, ehn, Belema? I know your stepmother doesn't give you money."

I told her to keep quiet and collect the money. The pain in her eyes was too much to bear. I would rather the anger I felt for Aunty Damaris eat me up than watch the only person that has been good to me suffer. When school closed, I dragged Shina to an empty class.

"I stole your money. It was me. I am sorry. I was angry at my aunty for how she has been treating me. I wanted to pay her back, so I stole your money. Shina, I am sorry for what I did. I didn't mean to hurt you. I will never do it again. Please don't stop being my friend.

You are the only person that cares for me. I am sorry," I spilled the word so fast I wasn't sure she heard all I said. I went on my knees. "Shina, please, I am sorry."

Tears were flowing down my cheeks. I never realized just how much I needed her love, needed her attention to help me get through each day. I was too broken. Losing her would undo the last thread of sanity holding me together.

"Get up," she said. She hugged me tight. We both cried like children that we were. That day, we signed a pact to be there for one another.

"I understand what you are going through. You will be fine. God would take care of you."

God did take care of me, but he didn't help me take care of Dad. Shina started to bring more food for both of us. She introduced me to her mother who took me as her second daughter. She sent snacks and drinks through Shina to me. My life was looking up until Dad fell ill. And then he recovered. And then I unknowingly disobeyed Aunty Damaris. And the full wrath of my father fell on me.

Since my stepmom stopped giving me meat and left me hungry on some days, I started to not care for school snacks. Some days, she would give me biscuits. Other days, she would not give me breakfast. I didn't complain because there was Shina to feed me.

One day, after I had finished my morning chores, taken my bath, got dressed, and ate breakfast, I got my bag to leave for school. Breakfast was rice and stew. My plate of rice was meatless, even though there were large chunks of beef in the stew. I wolfed the food. It was small. I was late for school, so I asked Aunty Damaris for snacks. She didn't respond. She continued pressing her phone. I stood in the parlor for a while, waiting for her to say something, but she didn't. I stood for fifty-three seconds. And while I stood, the AC hummed twenty times. The WhatsApp notification beep on her phone sounded twenty-nine times. She giggled four times, called somebody an idiot three times.

"I am leaving, Ma," I said. I left the room without waiting for her reply. She wasn't going to say anything anyway.

I was close to the gate when Debby called out to me that my aunty was calling me. I ignored her. *Which aunty would call me? Did I not just leave Damaris at home some second ago?* Debby was always cracking and making silly jokes. *Shebi she is blind to see that I am late, abi*, I thought as I walked out of the gate. She doesn't know this kind of joke was not funny in the morning. Before I opened the gate, I gave Debby a *waka*. *Rubbish girl doesn't know when not to play.*

After completing my chores for the evening, I was in my room, trying to force my eyelids to close. I didn't have any assignments that day so I could sleep early. Of recent, Dad and I never saw face to face. He returned from work too late to find me awake. Even though some days I was awake, I was either too exhausted to lift my body off the bed, or too unconcerned with his return to go greet him. Most times, I didn't care.

On this day, he returned from work thirty minutes earlier than he did the whole week. It was a Thursday. I was on my bed, counting the number of ticks the clock made, fiddling with random numbers in my head when I heard him laugh heartily, something he only does with his wife. *This is good*, I thought. I normally would have slept off by the time he started eating, but today, I was wide awake. Sleep didn't come early. Then after the clinking of plates, the *hmms*, and *arghs* from the living room, I heard a knock on my door.

Instinctively, I knew something was wrong. I pretended to be asleep. I ignored the knocking. Dad knocked again, this time harder. He wanted to bring down the door with his knuckles. I, feigned yawning, took forever to get off the bed before opening the door. I yawned again in his face when I opened the door. I greeted him. He didn't respond. He looked at me like I had horns sprouting out of my head. I greeted again, hoping my louder greeting would jolt him from whatever trance he was in. He didn't answer. Instead, he slapped me on the face. I felt my cheekbones shift. The teeth on my left cheek gave way. Something tore inside my mouth, and I started bleeding. I coughed blood as I bent my face away from him. Blood spittle.

"Why did you disrespect my wife?" he asked. His eyes were brewing with rage, so intense I knew I was dead meat. I wanted to call Grandma to tell her to prepare my grave and get an epitaph for me. I wanted her to prepare a speech that would be read at my funeral.

Living with the man whose sperm created me was the worst mistake I ever made. Even my absent mother's neglect is better than this man's love. I died in love. I died loving a man I should never have loved.

She would read it while tears streamed down her face. Dakumo will be there. She must be there. I miss her.

"To my room now!" he barked.

I obeyed without uttering a word. What could I even say? I was bleeding in the mouth, plus I didn't even know what I did. Even if I did, I was not going to explain myself away from the torture he was about to mete out on me, so I just obeyed. I was sheep at the slaughterhouse. Isaac! The sacrifice! Silence of the lamb!

His long koboko materialized. He scowled at me. His shirt was unbuttoned, the first five buttons. His trouser was rough in the middle, and the zip was opened. Three big blotches of sweat stain were on his shirt: one on his right arm, another at the back, and the biggest one on his chest. Counting the sweat stains helped me take my mind off what was about to happen.

"You have the guts to disrespect the woman that has been slaving out to take care of you?

Slay what? Is this man joking? I have been the one slaving out here, Father. I have been the one doing all the goddamn house chores.

"She called you when you were leaving for school, but you didn't answer her. You have grown too big in this house. You are growing"—he hit me on the head with the koboko—"wings abi?" He raised his hands to beat me again. I dodged the strike.

I had to explain myself. Now was the time. One. Two. Three. Your time starts now. You have five seconds. Make it count!

"I didn't know she was calling me. Debby told me she was calling me, but I thought she was joking, so I didn't answer her. I even gave Debby waka." I hurriedly spilled the words out of my mouth like hot oil. Hopefully, I hoped, it alleviates the anger and reduces the time he'll spend beating me. He didn't seem to have heard anything I said. He dragged me to the middle of the room, close to himself, and continued beating me. My subconscious mind began to speak again, you can never get used to pain. No matter how many times you have sex with pain, you can never understand what tickles it and when it orgasms.

The koboko knew the pathway on my body. It traced them easily, landing on places where it once traveled. The old koboko marks had not healed completely. The pain was, as the koboko struck old pathways, numbing. It stung me like a snake. The venom of his rage mixed with the thickness of the koboko and the sweat on my body was a powerful combination of pain-inflicting tools. I shouted for help. I knew it wouldn't come. Instincts.

"That is how you have been behaving, like a possessed witch in this house. You have been disrespecting your stepmom all these while." *Whip! Whip!* On my face. And back. And thighs. And head. He struck me with anger. The sting of the horsetail tore through my skin, into the core of my being. He dragged me by the hand to the bedside. I was curling and rolling away from him. He pinned me down to the bed with his legs tightly holding my flailing legs. His left hand grabbed my two hands and held them tight. With his free right hand, he whipped me on my face. The tail end of the koboko struck my eye, in the middle of my left eye.

"*Yee*! I am blind *ooh*!" I shouted with the last iota of strength I had left.

He let go off my hand now. He stood before my trembling curled body, towering over my brokenness.

"If you like, go blind, I will correct you, whichever way I can. I would not allow my daughter to become a nuisance. You think this discipline is too much, ehn? That is why"—he punched me on my stomach—"that is why you poisoned my food the other—" As if the anger had struck a bad chord, he dropped the koboko, looked at me with venom in his eyes. He was looking for something. His eyes scanned the room.

"Daddy, I didn't poison you," I manage to mutter between sobs and stabs of pain and anger.

Two days ago, he came home for lunch, and there were a few people in the house. His wife had just prepared vegetable soup and

OF LOVE AND BRUISES

garri. He was so famished that he ate hurriedly. At the third ball of garri, he started choking. I was asked to serve him water, and his wife hurriedly brought palm oil. She claimed it was a traditional antidote. How did he arrive at the conclusion that he was poisoned and not just choking? He felt better after digesting a few spoons of palm oil. No one spoke about what happened that day until today.

"You are still lying. You still have the guts to lie to me."

He dragged the bedspread from under my back. I rolled over to the other side of the bed.

He then pulled me to himself, threw the bedspread over me.

What is going on? What is this man doing this time?

He wanted to wrap me with the bedspread, but I was too big. Seeing the bedspread couldn't wrap all my body, he tied it around my head. He held on tight to the edge of the bedspread now over my head like a sack.

I was losing air fast.

"Why did you poison my food?" he asked.

"I didn't—" *Cough! Cough!*

The air in my lungs was quickly seeping out. I needed to breathe. I thrashed my hand this way and that, hoping to get a hold of the bedspread and take it off my face.

"Why do you want to kill me, ehn, Belema? Am I the first to have a child out of wedlock? Your mother is enjoying her life somewhere, and you want to make mine miserable."

I kicked and kicked, flapped my hands in every direction.

He wasn't letting go. He would allow me to choke to death if I kept on with my I-didn't-poison-you confession. I wasn't ready to be a martyr yet. There was Shina and Debby and Dakumo and the boy in JSS2 who still hasn't talked to me. There were these people to live for. I could not sacrifice myself on the altar of my father's wickedness, so like a prisoner being tortured at Guantanamo Bay I screamed,

"I did it," I managed to say between breathlessness. I had to admit to a crime I didn't commit because if I didn't, I don't know... I wasn't ready to die.

He removed the bedspread from my face. I sucked in air like a starving child scarves food. My eyes were beginning to turn to the back of my head. The pain on my body was nothing compared to the thought of dying from asphyxiation.

"What did you use to poison my food?"

"Spray polish."

Something had to give way. It was either I confessed to the crime, or be choked to death with a bedspread. I am very sure God would be disappointed in me when I get to heaven's gate, and I'm asked what killed me.

"Why the hell would you allow yourself to be killed with a bed-spread? Of all the things to be killed with," angry God would say, "you were killed with a cheap bedspread. How much is the bedspread?"

Ibinabo and Jack, My Fateful Comrades

The laborious whir of the ceiling fan filled the spaces in our conversations unsaid words should fill. We knew some things shouldn't be said, and we didn't bother saying them. Three of us were having an honest conversation in the living room, something that was impossible with Aunty Damaris around. She hated to see the three of us together. She knew we were up to no good. And she was right. Between the three of us, Jack, Ibinabo, and I, there was no stopping us when it came to doing the things parents don't approve of.

"Why does Francis always come here to do assignment?" Jack asked Ibinabo. Jack and Ibinabo were my cousins from my dad's side. They both came during the long holiday break. Dad informed me that Ibinabo would be staying with us because her mother couldn't take care of her. Her father, who she liked to call useless and stupid, had run away and left her mother alone with three children. Ibinabo, fifteen, left the house to stay with us to reduce the burden on her mother.

I was beyond elated when Dad told me Ibinabo and Jack would be coming to spend the holiday in our house. He explained that Jack would be staying only during the holidays, but Ibinabo would live with us for a while. Her father had run away, and her mother couldn't take care of her and her two siblings. I should be nice to her, he said. I should treat her like an older sister.

Tell your wife to be nice to her. I am not the bad one here.

Although I had never seen Ibinabo, I was super excited to meet her. Having an ally—and if Jack came, two allies—against Aunty Damaris was priceless. At least I would have somebody to gossip with and talk to. Ibinabo arrived two days earlier than Jack. She had the fairest skin I had ever seen. She was as tall as Dad, had thin lips, and a flat nose. Her ears were small, the type you can nibble on for days. She had deep-set eyes with full breast. They were as round, beneath the white polo she wore to the house that day, as Aunty Damaris's own. I was fascinated by the brightness of her smile, how her white teeth gleamed like the world were a fairy tale. She was genuinely happy. I had never seen a person so happy and full of life. She was wearing black jean trousers that day with one of her Ghana-must-go bags on the one hand and a black handbag on the other hand. Dad ordered me to bring her luggage from the boot. After Aunty Damaris pecked my dad, she went back to the book she was reading. She acted as if Ibinabo were invisible.

I hauled the two small bags of clothes and one bag that contained some foodstuffs into the house. Ibinabo's mum, in a show of gratitude, had given Dad some tubers of yam, plantain, and a small bag of garri. I arranged the foodstuffs in the kitchen, kept her bag in my room, and told her where the bathroom was. I also told her some simple rules of the house: wake early to do house chores, don't question Aunty Damaris, never ask for more food, respect Aunty Damaris like she was the goddess of the sea, and don't make Aunty Damaris angry. In all you do, never make her angry. And the last one, Dad beats a lot.

"That woman, your stepmother, what is wrong with her?" she whispered in my ear when we entered the room. I was helping her arrange her clothes in the wardrobe.

"What do you mean? What did she do?"

"Why is she acting like she is possessed? She acted as if she did not see me. Is that how she behaves?"

I liked her already—somebody to help me with my Aunty Damaris's troubles.

"That is how she is o. She is an angry lioness. If you want to enjoy your stay in this house, in all that you do," I dragged my right ear, "never offend her."

"Hian! Na wa o. What kind of a person always wears a frown? Doesn't she know too much frowning would make her face age quick? Wrinkles would riddle her face?"

"Does she care? She would buy cream to cover the wrinkles."

"Ehen! She uses cream!"

"Very well!"

"E go well be that."

I was asking her questions about her life and family and what she liked while she changed into a new cloth. I asked her about her clothes that I liked the one she just took off. She said my body was not good for the trouser that it was too big for me. As we talked, Jack entered the room and hailed the both of us. This was his second vacation with us. While I shook his hand, Ibinabo gave him a glance, then faced me.

"You ask too many questions o, Belema. I don't see you asking your stepmother questions like this." She was out of her jeans. She had a thin waistline and a wide hip.

"I don't talk to her at all o. That one, if I say anything, she will knock me or beat me, or if she wants to be the real devil that she is, she will report me to my father and that one is worse."

Ibinabo stood from the bed and was going to the bathroom when Jack asserted, "Hope you know that Francis is our neighbor, and he has no reason coming to our house."

"He doesn't know anything na that is why he is always here," Ibinabo replied. She twisted her braid and entered the bathroom. We heard her flush the toilet and come out.

"And you are Albert Einstein, right?" Jack asked when Ibinabo sat down.

"You know I am smart like that. You sef know say my head dey hot," she replied.

"Ibinabo, you know this boy and his mother's troubles. Hope you also know he is still in secondary school. This lesson you are teaching him that is not academic—" Jack stopped short. He looked from Ibinabo to me. I could tell from the way he bit his lips that he was holding back words. I had a fair idea of what was going on, but I could not and would not talk. Seeing the tension in the room had increased a few notches, he tried to crack a joke.

"I know say this your head is as hot as chimney—smoking. Is that why you keep giving him—"

"Guy, behave yourself na," Ibinabo cut Jack short. "You know the walls have ears. If these walls hear this rubbish you are about to say, don't you know it could get to the ears of another person. There are mysteries you will never understand."

"Oh, you know what you are doing is rubbish, don't you?" Jack asked, smiling at her. I couldn't contribute to this discussion because I didn't know how it would affect my biscuits and sweets. I couldn't sacrifice my salary.

"Dude, you have started to interfere with matters that don't concern you. You should start minding your business. All these your chor chor, gossip, will not help you." She gestured with her mouth bunched forward.

"I hope say you no go do this boy kill am. You know say you are crazy."

The weird relationship between Ibinabo and Francis, our neighbor downstairs, started two days after Dad opened a provision store for Aunty Damaris.

Aunty Damaris leaves the house in the morning and returns in the evening to make dinner for her husband. She always made sure she gave us enough work to last us the whole day.

"Jack, sweep my room. After you finish, go and buy gas for the house. Belema, wash your dad's trousers, wash my panties and bras, and sweep the parlor. Ibinabo, cook yam porridge and bring it to the shop. I don't want to come back and meet this house dirty o. Belema, make sure you mop everywhere. If that kitchen has a single stain on it, your father would hear." On and on she went, dishing out chores.

Meanwhile, Ibinabo was always at home, teaching Francis his assignment that he never finished. We were on holiday, so you could imagine the type of assignment a fifteen-year-old girl and a short

OF LOVE AND BRUISES

seventeen-year-old boy with a head too big for his innocent-looking face was doing.

I was at the door, seated, looking around, checking to see if anybody was coming. I was munching away at my reward—biscuits and sweet—for being the security guard. The compound was quiet that day. All the days I've watched the door while Ibinabo and Francis do their assignments, nobody ever came to the house. As it was, I was getting paid for doing nothing. It was a good job. I was, however, going to earn my pay that day.

As usual, the coast was clear. Francis came with his notebook, a pen, and other necessary learning tools. He wore his favorite faded Chelsea jersey with *Lampard* at the back. The *Lam* had washed off, leaving only *pard* at the back. Jack often joked that he comes to the house to play games with his *pad*. I was sitting there, licking my stick sweet, savoring the sweetness of it when I saw Dad coming out of his car. I was too caught up in my head to notice when he drove in. My chest began to beat fast. Danger! Danger! I didn't have enough time to run inside to inform Ibinabo of the incoming danger. So I started to knock on the door very hard many times to tell her that our biggest fear was coming to fruition. After about ten hard hitting, I walked outside to welcome Dad. I hid the chair I was sitting on. If Dad saw it, he'd know something was up.

Dad and I walked inside to meet Ibinabo and Francis bent over a book, studying. They had cleared out every trace of their earlier study.

"Welcome, uncle," Ibinabo said, calm and collected like it was a normal day, as if strange things hadn't been happening earlier.

Dad didn't respond. Francis looked up from the book and greeted Dad.

I stood behind Dad with his bag in my hand, hoping beyond hope that he didn't notice anything. If he did, if he knew what was going on, I was in deep trouble, and Ibinabo, in a hotter pot of soup. He walked into his room. I followed behind.

"Who is that boy in my living room?" he asked as soon as I walked into his room.

"He is Ibinabo's friend," I said in the calmest voice I could muster. I hoped he didn't sense the trembling beneath my answer.

"I don't want to see him in this—" He stood from the bed. His stockings were off, his shirt was unbuttoned, and he had unbuckled his belt. "I need to talk to him. I don't want to ever see him in my house again."

He went to the sitting room, warned Francis sternly never to come to his house again. If he saw him, Dad threatened, he would cut off his penis and feed it to his parents as pepper soup. Francis wanted to protest that he was only studying with Ibinabo, but she tugged at his shirt for him to keep his mouth shut.

"That Francis is a stupid boy o. He wanted to defend the lie he was telling in front of uncle," she said the next day when the three of us were having our night amebo session. We all slept in the same room.

Francis never showed up again. We all heaved a sigh of relief that night during our amebo session. Jack and Ibinabo were impressed with my security skills. I would make a good detective. I should seriously consider being one, Jack advised. I blushed. It felt good to be praised and appreciated for something I did. When was the last time somebody aside from Shina told me I did something right? I reveled in the praise for two days until Uncle Preye showed up.

Uncle Preye was my dad's half-brother. He was on a semester holiday at his university, so he decided to spend two weeks with us. He was studying philosophy at the University of Port Harcourt. He was older than all of us. I think he was around twenty-three. His full beards and lean frame didn't do justice to his boyish face. He looked eighteen. Maybe that was why Ibinabo liked him. I don't know what it was, but Ibinabo warmed up to him, forgetting he was her uncle.

Their relationship was suspicious from the start. The way Ibinabo laughed at his jokes when he came to our room. The way she moved around him, always whining her waist for him to take note. The agbaya sef was not helping matters, licking his lips whenever she passed him in the living room. He used a lot of sexual innuendos with her. He bought her perfume on his fourth day of staying with us. I knew he was trouble, and my fears were confirmed a week after.

Aunty Damaris and I went to the photographer's shop to snap passport photos. Aunty Damaris needed the passport to get a loan from the bank. When we returned from the photographer's shop, the house felt different. Although things looked like nothing happened, Uncle Preye was watching football on Super Sports. Ibinabo was in the kitchen, making lunch for everybody. There was an air that I could not understand. Jack was in our room. He didn't go out to play that day.

As soon as I entered the room, Jack started laughing. His laugh was saying something he wasn't saying.

"Jack, what is it? Why are you laughing like a fool?" I inquired. The sound of football commentary seeped into the room.

"Belema, don't worry. I am fine."

"I know. Say something is up. You can't just be laughing without a reason. Jack, tell me something. I am your person."

He continued laughing and started to sing Asa's classic, "Fire on the Mountain."

"Please. What fire?" I asked. I sat on the bed, waiting for Jack to finish his singing and tell me what was going on. I banked on our closeness for him to spill the beans. Being two years older than him, I was closer to him than I was with Ibinabo.

"I can't tell you anything. You wey your mouth no fit close. By the time your dad starts beating you, you go just froor like water water shit."

"Abeg na. I won't tell anybody," I pleaded with him. While Jack boasted in his ability to keep whatever secrets he was told, I was the direct opposite. I could not help myself from spilling secrets. All you need to do is beat me. I hated cane so much, I could sell my birthright if I were threatened with a cane to sell it.

"The thing wey my ears hear, the thing wey my eyes see, I no fit talk am."

Ibinabo entered the room. Her hand was wet, and she was sweating. She was making jollof rice for the family.

"Ibinabo, do you by chance know what is causing Jack to laugh like a jackass?" I asked her. I was hoping she would use our girl code to communicate the secret to me. She laughed and told me not to pay any mind to Jack.

"Don't mind him. That is how he acts like an idiot." She changed into a cropped top and left the room.

I kept prodding the laughing Jack for answers until he budged.

"I will tell you," he whispered. Our door was closed. "But when I tell you, I don't want to hear it outside o. Make another ear no hear am oo!"

"No ear go hear am. Why are you laughing?"

"Shey you see that your uncle wey siddon for parlor so?"

"Ehn, what is wrong with him?"

"That your uncle is a real bad guy."

"What did he do?"

"Belema, your uncle Preye, dey chop—" He looked at the door as if somebody was going to burst through it the moment he said the secret.

"That your uncle dey chop Ibinabo kpomo."

I pretended like I didn't understand what he meant by kpomo. With information such as the one he was telling, clarity was of importance. You don't want to get misinformed and start running around with assumptions. Assumptions didn't make the amebo sweet.

"What does kpomo mean? What is he doing with Ibinabo?"

"Belema! Belema!" he complained. "You know nothing at all."

"Agreed. What did Preye do to Ibinabo?"

"Preye dey knack Ibinabo akpako. Preye is having sex with Ibinabo."

"I swear, Jack, you are mad! That isn't possible, and you know it. Why would you make a joke of something this serious?"

I knew it was true, but I had to pretend for a while, form surprise. In the ambo underworld, ignorance gets your informant excited. And when your informant is happy, you get the juicier story, for free.

Jack then unraveled the marvel to me. He was lost in the movie on his phone as soon as we left. Uncle Preye and Ibinabo, seeing how consumed he was with his phone and how long he was going to spend with the phone, decided to have a quick one. It seemed they had been doing it before but didn't last as long as what they had that day. Jack was hungry. He stopped the movie on his phone and noticed the house was eerily quiet. He went to the living room. Nobody was there. Where were Ibinabo and Uncle Preye? Maybe they went to get something. He wanted to enter the kitchen. The door was closed. Strange.

The kitchen door is never closed that is why there is a curtain. His instinct told him something was up. He went closer to the door, put his ear on the door, and then he heard the slow suppressed moan of Ibinabo. Jack listened for a few more minutes, trying to be sure what he heard was no imagination that his curious mind hadn't weaved it into reality. It was true. He said he went back to the room as if nothing happened. Ibinabo entered a few minutes later, her face neat and innocent like nothing happened. She asked how the movie Jack was watching was going, and Jack, being the idiot that he is, said it was sweet. The "*sweet*" slurred. Ibinabo knew he knew.

"That was how she said, 'Jackie, you go tell uncle wetin happen?'" Jack said while he twisted his black earpiece. He was enjoying telling the story.

"I promised to keep the secret with me till I die. The only issue I have is that Preye guy," Jack continued.

"And what is the problem?"

"I no trust am at all. There is something spooky, fishy, cunning. There is something deceptive about him."

"I know. But what can we do?"

"We can show him small pepper na."

"But it would affect Ibinabo."

"I no trust Preye. Belema, be careful around him o. With that him big eyes like Titus fish own so. Shey you see as him leg curve like that pole for Granada junction?"

We both started to laugh at the joke when the door flung open. We stopped our laughter, shocked at the face staring down at us— Aunty Damaris.

"I have been calling you since to go and help Ibinabo in the kitchen, but you didn't answer. What is happening here? Ibinabo is tired. She needs you in the kitchen," Aunty Damaris bellowed. She always shouts whenever she was angry.

As soon as Aunty Damaris said "Ibinabo is tired," Jack and I started laughing. In my mind—and I am sure that was the same thought that ran through Jack's mind—I said, "Why she no go tired after all the things she has been doing?" Jack and I looked at each other and increased the intensity of our laughter. We were speaking to ourselves in unspoken language, the language of the initiated.

We forgot Aunty Damaris was there. The hilarity of the situation was too intense for us not to laugh.

"Una dey use me laugh, abi?"

"Aunty, no o. No be like that." Jack was trying to control his fits of laughter. He held his stomach as he talked.

"Jack, why are both of you laughing? What is going on?"

I left the room to avoid Aunty Damaris asking me any questions.

"She threatened to report us to your father for laughing at her," Jack told me later.

"It is not a threat. She will do it."

Aunty Damaris took our laughing to heart. She thought we were laughing at her and so wanted to take revenge.

"What do we do now? When my dad returns, he would use cane to settle the matter. He won't even ask for our side of the story."

"No problem. I no dey fear cane. Which kind mumu cane person wan use beat me wey go pain me. As I don promise Ibinabo say nothing go make me commot this secret from my belly, nothing fit happen. The problem we have now is you. Can you keep your mouth closed when the lashes start coming? Can you hold a secret?"

"I would not say anything," I assured him. I knew it was a lie. I will spill the truth if the beating got too intense for me. And my dad knew how to beat the words out of me, lie or truth. He could conjure them with the right number of strokes.

When I heard my father's thunderous voice, I knew the time had come. I steeled myself for what laid ahead. I kept muttering self-belief mantras to myself, telling myself I had it within me to keep my mouth shut. "I had to do this for Ibinabo," I told myself. Although as I walked from my room to my father's, fear tightened the air in my chest. Still, I wore a brave face. I reminded myself of how the secret Dad was asking was not one to be spilled. "I would keep my mouth shut. I would keep my mouth shut," I muttered these words to myself almost a thousand times before I entered my father's room.

But those words couldn't stop me from spilling the beans like a careless three-year-old. I tried, really, I tried. I didn't want to tell Dad anything, although I knew the sting of the whip was going to tear me. I honestly thought I could withstand it, having seen Jack leave with his head held high.

Jack winked at me when I finally entered my father's room. The journey from my room to his was hellish. Jack brushed me slightly on the shoulder. I guess it was his own way of telling me to keep the secrecy flag flying, to hold on till the end. But only if he knew I was not like him. Only if he knew that I could never get used to beating the way he did. If he knew I was not as strong as him.

I stood before my father and his wife with hot pee slowly seeping into my panties. The look in his eyes, the evil stare his wife shot at me, the hotness of the room, the silence in the room when I entered. Everything was conspiring to drag the secret out of my mouth. And I tried to keep the words locked in.

"Ask Belema. She was laughing with Jack," Aunty Damaris said to my father. He held the whip in his left hand. Pretty strange because he flogged with his right hand. With his shirt off, and beads of sweat dripping from his body, I knew Jack had received his own share of the beating but hadn't budged. *I, too, can do it.*

"Belema, why were you and Jack laughing?" Dad asked in a rather-calm tone. The calm before the beating.

"Nothing, Dad. We were laughing at something else. We were not laughing at aunty. It was something different."

"I know. So what was the different something you were both laughing at if it wasn't my wife?"

"Erm, Daddy, it's not like that—"

I didn't know when he sprung to his feet, walked to where I was standing with my head bowed and heart thumping with fear.

Tawai! Whip! Whip!

The koboko hit my skin in quick successions I didn't know when I sputtered "Ibinabo and Uncle Preye." I was tired of getting beat. My body was beginning to lose its name, its identity, with each stroke that kissed it. I wanted no more of it. I was done giving my body hell just because I was his child. I needed to rest. If Ibinabo and Preye (I stopped calling him Uncle Preye since the day he brushed his hand against my bum. The brushing, as he said, mistakenly stayed too long.) wanted to act like idiots. That was their problem. My body won't be penance for other people's sins.

"What did Preye and Ibinabo do?"

"Erm, they did not do anything o. It was a slip of the tongue."

He flogged me with the koboko again. This time, he targeted my neck and waist. He knew the weakest parts of my body, having explored all the hidden pathways and secret corals with his whip. Where I screamed the most, where I held the longest, where I felt nothing. Dad knew which part of my rock he should strike if he wanted water and oil and tears and gold and diamond. He had the map on his palms.

"Both of them are—" I was stammering because I didn't want to betray the only person—Ibinabo—whom I could freely talk with. She would hate me after this, never talk to me again. Which was better? Saving my body from purgatory, or saving for heaven Ibinabo's friendship. My body needed saving. I chose it.

"Ibinabo and Preye have an affair. They are having sex," I managed to mutter. Time took a backflip, moonwalked, and stopped. Silence. Stunned beyond words, my dad dropped the koboko. Aunty Damaris dropped her hands on her lap. Twenty ticktocks of the clock later, Dad stood up, tightened his belt around his waist. Without taking his eyes off the ground, he ordered Aunty Damaris to get Cameroon pepper. His voice was hollow like it was lost in a deep well, and he was searching for it. Dad was broken. Never had I seen his face fall and make a pool of pain. He gathered the courage still left in him, stormed out of the room, and banged the door.

"Ibinabo!" he barked as he left the room. His voice filled the 8 p.m. darkness. Ibinabo came out of the room, defiant in her look, obviously not giving a damn. She kept a straight face—no emotion.

"Where is that idiot Preye?" he continued, his feet thumping against the tiles. Preye jolted from the sofa in the living room. He was watching a movie on Africa Magic, rare for him. He often said Nigerian movies were bland and lacked imagination. According to him, there was little, or nothing one can learn from Nigerian movies. Guess the tension of his impending punishment, one he would never have imagined, led him to seek succor and hope in a bland boring Nigerian film.

"Preye, what have you been doing in my house?" After switching off the TV, Dad sat on the couch, fuming with anger.

"Uhm, Uncle," Preye wanted to say something, maybe deny what happened, but he thought against it. He knew trying to defend himself would only fan the already-volcanic flames of my father's anger. He dropped his stare to the ground. I was by the door of our room. Jack and I were watching the drama. Ibinabo stood, arms folded across her chest, eyes to nowhere. Aunty Damaris was with a Bama bottle, half-filled with black pepper. Cameroon pepper was the deadliest of them all when it comes to pepper. It was what we used to make pepper soup when Dad wanted his tongue to burn with pepper. Nobody eats Cameroon pepper in a plate of food and not sweat and drink gallons of water afterward. One spoonful could cook full-party jollof rice and still be peppery.

"Is that Cameroon pepper I see with Aunty Damaris?" Jack asked. His voice hushed to avoid annoying Dad more.

"I think so. Dad asked her to get pepper for him."

"Jesus! Na, so your father wicked?"

"You never see anything."

"And, you, madam, wey don dey see wetin she no suppose see, would you get those stupid knees on the ground before I strangle you by myself?"

Ibinabo reluctantly knelt.

"I don't know what got into both of you, but you would not disgrace me in this house. You would not bring shame to my family and me. Both of you have no common sense to know that this nonsense you did is wrong. Are you too stupid to think?"

Nobody said anything. NEPA seized power. Darkness. Dad turned on the light on his phone. Aunty Damaris followed suit.

"Ibinabo, your father is nowhere to be found. Your mother is struggling to keep the clothes on her back and that of your two siblings from turning into tatters and cover their nakedness. She is struggling to put food, at least a square meal, on the table for your siblings, and all you can think about is how you want to fuck?"

This was the first time he was using explicit words. He was always so formal and serious.

"You think say na fuck dey put money for hand? Abi e dey put food for table? You just wan waste your life abi, Ibinabo? You want to waste your life?" He stretched the koboko. He asked Jack to put on the generator that we called "*I better pass my neighbor.*"

"As I dey talk so, if you don't strip naked ehn, I go do you something wey be say if your mama come look for you, she no go recognize you again."

"So you don't have sense enough to know that this girl is an underage? At your old age, even with your education, you allowed your penis to get the best of you. Fool! Do you know you just had sex with an underage? Shey you know say I fit arrest you for this thing wey you do? C'mon, strip before I tear your trouser myself."

Preye nodded.

Ibinabo, reluctant at first, was taking off her clothes. She was wearing only panties and a bra.

"I said you should take off all your clothes. Were you deaf? Take off those things, my friend."

She glared at Dad. She unhooked the straps of her bra. Aunty Damaris stood by the corner. A glint of fulfillment filled her eyes. She liked what was happening. "Devil! She would burn in hell," Jack said when he saw her smiling.

Her bra, undone, revealed breasts that forced dad to lower his head before bringing them to focus again. Her breast was big for her age. She took off her white panties. Stubbles of pubic burst into view. Naked, Ibinabo was a goddess. The glint in Aunty Damaris's eyes faded. Jealousy clouded her eyes. Preye was also naked at this point.

"Get me one sachet of pure water there."

Dad collected the pure water from Aunty Damaris, opened it, and poured its content on Ibinabo and Preye. Ibinabo wanted to protest. I could see it in her body movement, in the way she shrugged when the cold water touched her skin. But she didn't. She couldn't. When the roof over your head is held by a man who takes pleasure in abusing you physically, the only protest you can make is telling your body to still itself for whatever happened. Because, to be honest, a homeless body is worse than one riddled with temporary pain and koboko marks. Pain can be understood, but homelessness can't. It exposes your body and soul and mind to all the harsh elements of weather and the demons in men's clothing lurking in dark street corners and broad daylight.

She stayed calm, didn't blink, or said a word. She reminded herself, I imagined, that there was nothing she could not handle, no beating too intense.

I guess the kind of punishment that awaited her at the hands of a man who believed he was closer to God in righteousness was something her mind would never have fathomed. But my dad had a penchant for creativity, even if it was creativity in meanness and being evil.

He ordered Jack and me to come out and tie Ibinabo's hands. Preye said nothing. He dared not. Jack dragged his feet. I think he knew what was going to happen.

"Jack, get me a rope from my car. It is in my car, at the back seat." He threw his car keys to Jack who caught it deftly and went outside to fetch the rope.

"E go be today. The unimaginable would happen today," Jack whispered to me before he left the sitting room. We both knew the night could not have gotten any darker for Ibinabo.

When Jack returned with the thick black rubber rope, I saw fear in his eyes, deeply seated fear. Dad ordered Jack to form a knot with the rope.

Jack did. He gave it to my dad who then wound it around Ibinabo's outstretched arm. She was prepared for the worse. He drew both ends of the rope, and the knot tightened around her arm. He did the same for her legs. Ibinabo was bound and stuck. She couldn't free herself from the pain if and when the pain became unbearable. That is what Dad is good at—keeping you trapped while he meted out his punishment to you. He didn't believe in freedom. Jack did the same on Preye's legs and hands. Only this time, he made it much tighter. He really wanted Preye to suffer more.

He commanded Ibinabo to splay on the floor. She did as she was told. Then he collected the bottle of pepper from his wife, opened the bottle, and used a plastic spoon to scoop a spoonful. He bent over the naked and splayed Ibinabo, his eyes trained on her wet vagina. He pinched some pepper with his other hand and started to sprinkle them over her vagina. I shut my eyes tight when Ibinabo let out a deafening cry. I knew that pain. I have lived inside that kind of pain room before. It is dark, airless, and filled with nails on every side of the wall. You can't turn in that room. You were stuck. Your cries were wrapped in many languages, like a collage of unknown tongues.

Dad didn't care. He kept sprinkling the pepper on her vagina. Ibinabo continued screaming, trying to wriggle free from the rope. Jack did a perfect job. She couldn't wiggle them off.

Dad proceeded to rub her wet body with pepper, after he had put enough pepper inside her vagina. I could have imagined her clitoris was burning like hell. I can imagine the tearing sensation, like a hot knife snaking inside her. I could imagine how she turned inside the room filled with nails. I imagined she couldn't stay still any longer. I imagined she was turning to the left, getting pierced by the nails, and when she turned to the right, there was another piercing. She was bleeding. She was losing air. I could only close my eyes and hope Dad was not mad. (Because saying he'll come to his sense was out of the question. He was in his right sense inflicting pain on a teenage girl.) He has to stop the madness. I prayed that God, wherever he was, if he existed at all, should strike my dad with madness, or stroke, or any type of sickness to stop him from continuing his atrocity on Ibinabo.

God remained silent. *Does he even listen before? Dude has been quiet since I came here.*

NEPA restored power. It was 8:45 p.m. I wanted to go to my room. I couldn't stand the sight. I was walking out of the living room while Dad started rubbing pepper on Preye when Aunty Damaris asked, "Belema, where you dey go?"

Idiot! Would you mind your business and stop acting like the witch that you are? Don't you have human sympathy, or has your heart been replaced with stone? Witch! Beg your husband to stop.

"I want to go and change over. Light has come."

"Good. When you are done, come back and watch so you, too, don't go around fucking family members like a prostitute." She said the fucking with venom, with the highest timbre of hatred one could ever muster. *Today was explicit-words day, so go on, witch, use fucking as you want.*

Dad picked up his koboko. I saw the rage devour him. He was going to beat Ibinabo and Preye with their body wet and coated in pepper. He was going to whip them like slaves. This was his most creative punishment yet. And in that moment, as he unbuttoned his shirt, as he did his customary koboko stretch, I knew that I, too, was going to suffer this fate. He saw, just like I did and every other person there, that this punishment was lethal, that it was yielding the desired result: pain that numbed.

He raised his hands, struck the deadliest first whip I had ever seen. That first strike instantly tore Ibinabo's skin. Ibinabo's voice was losing its intensity, going hoarse after crying for too long. But that first strike brought out the sound from wherever they had been resting, exhausted. The yelp tore through the core of my consciousness, and it did Aunty Damaris's too. Aunty Damaris winced while Jack closed his ears with his hands. Dad remained unflinching.

Okay, now you are officially the devil. Who doesn't feel pain after this kind of cry? Who won't cringe and try to hold back himself from disintegrating into salty tears themselves after this kind of painful cry? I hate you now! You are officially a dead man with no human feelings. Go to hell, devil! Go to the bottomless parts of hell and burn with your demons! This world isn't yours! Leave us alone. And please take your demonic wife along with you! While at it, make sure you drag her screeching body along with you.

Dad continued to flog them all over their body. Ibinabo, in mind-numbing pains, rolled from one corner of the parlor to the next, hands and legs still tied. Dad followed her and kept flogging her. Meanwhile, the fool who slept with her was trying to be a man. Sadly, the blend of the pepper on new open wounds, receiving several kisses from Dad's koboko every two seconds, was too much for the man in him to endure. He was apologizing, but at this point, his words meant nothing. It was like Nigerians constantly begging Buhari to fix the economy and then receiving more policies that cause hardship. Still, he didn't stop apologizing.

Ibinabo's voice lost its energy as the koboko drew blood from her skin. Her rolling to avoid the pelting reduced drastically as the map of pain formed fully. Then fifteen minutes later (I fixed my eyes on the clock to avoid looking at the carnage my father was engineering), Ibinabo stopped rolling, stopped crying. She stopped trying.

She had slipped into the other room. I have been in that room so many times, my name was inscribed on its walls. I was sure Ibinabo would see my name on the walls. She went eerily quiet. Dad flogged her a few times, but when he saw there was no reaction from her, he stopped.

"Damaris, come here!" Even when he was in trouble, my father still sounded commanding, always the boss in charge of everything.

Be in charge now, boss. Be in charge of the death of your family. Kill your niece and own it with your fucking chest.

Aunty Damaris, who had been wearing a wide grin all the while, lost the light. She, too, knew what the consequences were. She hurried to the lifeless body, bent over her, ear to her chest, looking for a pulse.

"I think she is still breathing, even though faintly." Aunty Damaris was sent to school to be trained as a nurse, but she was too uninterested, in her own words, to continue. Dad believed she must have learned something.

"Hurry. Get water. Let's sprinkle it on her face." His voice had the tiny tremor of an earthquake, unsure whether it wants to happen or not.

Jack and I ran over to Ibinabo's body as soon as Aunty Damaris went to get water from the kitchen.

Dad sprinkled water over Ibinabo's face. Her face was losing color. Dad saw it. His fear began to crawl into his voice.

"She's not responding, Damaris. What is wrong? I thought you said you heard a pulse?"

"Yes, I did. Keep pouring the water."

I was too afraid to wait for the stupid sprinkling to work. I got a cup of water and, without warning, without thinking about anything, emptied the water on Ibinabo's face. I was desperate. I wanted her alive. I needed her back. She was the only person who understood me.

Cough! Cough! Cough! Cough!

Ibinabo coughed back to life. Nothing happened to Preye. He didn't pass out. He left the house the next day. No goodbyes, nothing. He disappeared like a ghost that never visited.

Unlearning the Meaning of Love

....

When the cloud above a home has turned gray, the sun loses its sight, goes blind, and wears the cloak of indifference. Our house, after the horrendous experience Ibinabo suffered, after her healing that took the whole of one month of laying helplessly on the bed, after her stubbornness increased and her skin turned steel against the beatings and rebukes, after she started to care less about what my father thought and was at the fuck-you-all stage of her life, felt like a graveyard with living corpses. I turned to myself to find joy.

Resumption was still far, and I knew deep down that I had lost a part of myself with Ibinabo. She didn't blame me for her predicament. Never did. She understood the pressure I was under that day, the things I had been going through, and from then onward, she looked at me differently. She protected me, cared for me. She became a big sister to me.

Jack left two weeks after Ibinabo's pummeling. He said to us on the day of his departure, "I wish you all the best. I could never have imagined the kind of hell you were living in, Belema. This place is hell."

"But your house, from the stories you told us, is not any better. Isn't that how you got your rock-thick skin? Don't they beat you as often, even more than they do here?" I was desperately looking for hope, trying to clutch at imaginary optimism straws to help me stay sane. Ibinabo's beating made me realize how much of an endangered species I was and how my body, too, like Ibinabo's, would be subjected to the same torture.

"Yes, the beating in my house is regular. One day like that, my father beat me with the fan belt of an Okada because I went to play football. He would not listen to my explanation. He beat me so much I lost consciousness, just like Ibinabo. But he would never use pepper and water on my private part. He would never drag my naked self around the street. Never."

Sharing tales of our lives with wicked and disciplinary parents filled most of our night conversations. The three of us started to learn just how much of a torture dungeon our houses were. While Ibinabo didn't have the koboko-littered and cane-filled home as Jack and I had, hers was more of psychological abuse. Her mother abused her, reduced her worth to nothing but a vagina. She is ugly, her mother would tell her. She was a spitting replica of her father and a useless thing.

Ibinabo's Becoming

....

Ibinabo, on a hot night, narrated to us how she became what she was. It was supposed to be a harmless conversation about school and our neighbors. But when Jack said he wished Ibinabo and I lived in his house so we could better understand why cane had nothing on him, Ibinabo laughed at him.

That day's heat was intense. Ibinabo was wearing a bra and a bum shorts. Jack wore a yellow singlet with tiny holes at the base. I was shirtless. It was ten at night. Our transformer, according to rumors from neighbors, was bad. NEPA needed two months to fix it. We were into day two of the blackout. We later discovered that the rumor was bogus. Nothing was bad. NEPA just acted like NEPA.

"You think torture is only the beatings you receive? Do you know how much pain I went through in my mother's house? Do you—" She started crying. I never thought I would see the day Ibinabo would cry.

Jack shifted from his side on the bed and wrapped his hands around Ibinabo.

"Ibinabo, I was not trying to diminish whatever you suffered. It was only a joke. We are not on trial for who-suffer-pass Olympics na," Jack added jokingly.

"I understand wetin you dey talk, Jack. But I think it is best I explain to you guys why I do the things I do. Two of you are the closest people I have to a family. You deserve to know."

And so she started.

"Growing up, my mother never beat me as much as your dad, but she didn't help me either. Every mistake I made earned me curses and a reiteration of just how stupid and useless I was. She constantly called me ashawo, prostitute, whenever she saw me talking to boys. I was twelve when my mother, enraged that I burnt the small egusi soup she wanted us to manage for the week, told me to go and meet "my ashawo friends." Ibinabo cracked a thin smile. I could sense the memories were ripping her apart. I wanted her to stop talking. The pain was palpable.

"She said I had better go and bring money for her to make another soup, else I won't sleep in her house," Ibinabo continued. "What kind of a godforsaken child did God even give her? She would lament. She didn't think of what I would do to get money. She wanted me to get money and that was it. How I got it was my problem." I saw Jack shift uncomfortably on the bed. He rubbed his eyes with the heel of his palm. It was not sleep. It was the weariness of the pain we both knew awaited us. For Ibinabo to open up on something this deep, it meant there was something deeper ahead. We listened as Ibinabo kept on with her story.

"My mother sent me out that day to get money for food. I walked around the streets for almost an hour, confused and angry. My breast was forming then, not as big as this, but substantial enough to get the men and boys looking. After I had walked around the streets for a while, I remembered a lady who people often called ashawo in our area." Ibinabo fell silent for a while. The atmosphere was getting thicker. Nobody dared utter a word. We waited for her to collect herself and continue.

"This aunty liked me and was always telling me how beautiful I was," Ibinabo continued. "I used to ignore her because of her ashawo reputation, but that day, she looked like the only bright side to a dark tunnel. I found my way to her house. It was almost evening. I guessed my mother would be worried sick after her anger had cooled off. She might start to panic, scared something bad had happened to me. But I didn't care. I wanted to make her happy, even for a day. I got to this auntie's place, but she wasn't around. I was told she went to get something down the road and that I should wait. I sat on a bench close to her room. The other rooms were occupied by ladies in their midtwenties and early thirties who did a similar job as her. They didn't look like bad people—seeing them in their bum shorts and cropped tops, walking around the compound. They were friendly and smiled at me." I stood up to get a towel. We were sweating. I handed the towel over to Jack after I dabbed my head with it. He dried the sweat on his chest and passed the towel to Ibinabo. She collected it and dried her sweaty body. I wished NEPA would restore power. When she finished with the towel, Ibinabo continued with her story.

"Nothing about them was bad. I wondered why I had hated this aunty. They were ashawos, no doubt, but they were not evil. They did not treat me like a different person. When aunty arrived, she smiled and hugged me. She was genuinely happy to see me."

"She asked me what I was doing in her house at this time of the day, asked after my mother and two siblings. 'They are fine,' I responded, ;na just hunger dey beat them.' She unlocked her door, and we entered inside. Although her room was not as big, it was the neatest place I had ever seen. She had a plasma TV on her wall, wallpapers of forests, and random colors splashed on a canvass. Her sound system was heavy. Her bed filled more than half of the room with a green bed cover with prints of small children running around neatly tucked on the bed. The room smelled like baby powder, not like the fufu odor in our small room." I giggled when she said fufu odor. I knew that smell. Some of our neighbors in the village had that smell in their house. I hated it ehn.

"Two single-seater leather chairs were arranged opposite each other. She asked me to sit and offered me a glass of juice from her small fridge. I gulped the orange juice fast. She gave me another, and the juice met the same fate as the first glass." Jack licked his lips. Jack was a food monger.

"After I finished drinking a full Ragolis bottle of chilled water, I explained to her what had happened to me and how she was my last resort. She listened intently, gave me one thousand naira, and told me to see her again whenever I had the chance. I went back there two days later, hoping to get money. I wasn't sure why *aunty* should give me money, but I went. My mother's mood changed after the one thousand naira, and I wanted to keep it that way. I met her at home that day, and like the first time, she offered me orange juice. I did as before—gulped thirstily. I told her I needed her to introduce me to her business. I needed money to support my family and help me go to school." Ibinabo paused for a few seconds. The emotions were welling up now. I could sense it. The fan whirred slowly at first and then picked pace. Power had been restored. "Our sweaty bodies would dry now," Jack said. He was trying to dissipate some of the building emotions. I was close to tears now. I felt the pain in Ibinabo's voice grow like a cancerous mold.

"She said I was too young to do what she did, but she had another job for me to do. She then complimented me on my breast. She said that my breasts were beautiful and that it needed care and attention. I was shocked. My twelve-year-old mind didn't think any-thing of it." Ibinabo's voice melted into a soft whisper now. The pain was clawing its way to her throat.

"I sat there, waiting for her to explain," she continued. "She walked to me, took her hands, and rubbed my breast gently. I felt an electric current ripple through me like a faulty transformer. Lights sparked inside my body. I jolted at the touch. I liked the sensation that coursed through me, but I knew I could not allow myself to feel it. I focused on the noise coming from outside the room. Two ladies were laughing over a joke. The one with the loudest laugh was saying the man was a goat in between laughs. I liked the energy her laughter carried. I wanted that kind of carefree attitude, that kind of energy. I didn't like the energy inside me. The room was shrinking me. I was losing air, and I loved it. I know it was stupid but that was how I felt.

"Aunty told me that I was a beautiful girl and that she could make me rich. She said I didn't have to be a prostitute to be rich. She said, placing her hand on my shoulder, that I should be her baby. I would have all the good things of life if I agreed to make her happy."

"See, ehn, I wanted to remove her hand because I was begin-ning to understand what she was talking about, but I felt both great and scared. Her touch was heavenly, I will be honest, but the fear of what she was asking of me ripped me into shreds." The night was wearing off nicely now. Except the tears welling up in my eyes. And in Jack's. The story was not what we were expecting. It was not what

I was expecting. Jack went to the fan regulator to reduce the speed of the fan. The room was getting chilly. He just wanted to distract Ibinabo from continuing the story. We needed to catch our breath, control our emotions. We should not cry.

"Ladies like her, ladies who were into other ladies, were a taboo. I couldn't be seen with her. People will suspect. As if reading my head, she touched my face, pushed my head slightly to look up at her. 'Nobody will know. I will keep it a secret. You have nothing to fear,' Aunty said."

"I was taken to seventh heaven the moment her lips touched mine. Glued to the sofa, I didn't know what magic she used to get me naked. What she did to me to get me kissing her passionately. I kissed like I had always done it. It felt surreal but sweet. The things we did, God, they were beautiful." Jack licked his lips and cracked a smile. He knew how to let off tension. I sat there, transfixed by Ibinabo's story. Then smiled when Jack let out a funny sound. Ibinabo laughed. The first time since she started her story.

I left the room to the kitchen. I returned with a plastic bottle of chilled water and three plastic cups. I filled the cups with water. The three of us gulped the water. We waited for Ibinabo to continue her story. And she did after drinking the second cup of water.

"I became her baby, and she became my aunty. My mother didn't ask me how I was getting the money I brought to the house. She was comfortable with me leaving the house twice a week to stay with *aunty*. So long as money was on the table, Mama was good. The curses reduced. I was still going to school. I was in JSS3 then, and aunty encouraged me to study hard. She told me that if I studied hard enough and became a graduate, I will be able to take care of my family without needing to sleep with men like she did. She said she didn't like men. She was indifferent around them. According to her, sex with men was bland, nothing like what we had. Every week, we did different things with our bodies, explored every sex style known to man. She once complimented me on how fast I was learning. She said I was born a lesbian.

"I went to her house on one of my regular visits, and after a sumptuous meal of yam and egg sauce, she started telling me why I needed to stay with her.

"'See how you go down on me,' she said, 'I swear, no girl has ever gone down on me like that. The things you do, I swear, you be witch.'

"I basked in her compliments, and every time before I went to see her, I watched lesbian porn on websites she gave me. I wanted to please her. The wad of cash she was giving me was good—ten thousand naira on good weeks, less on bad ones. There was enough money for Mama and me. We were eating well.

"I didn't want her to stop giving me money, or to stop loving me. It was supposed to be me and her only, but her neighbors started to catcall me whenever I went to her place. I reported this to her. I thought she would condemn the act, promising to warn them against it. Instead, she told me to stop acting like a child.

"It was after steamy sex. We were still trying to catch our breath. There was no light, so she turned on her small generator.

"'We are all harlots, so why the shame?' she yelled. 'If my friends and neighbors call you, answer them. Abi you no wan make money? It seems like poverty hasn't dealt with you enough in this life. No dey do like pikin o. Open your eyes.' Her reply was shocking. I shrugged it off and thought nothing of it. Maybe she was angry at something. *She loved me*, I thought, *so there was no need overthinking things.*"

"What I had considered nothing was a big deal. On my next visit, she told me two of her friends were going to be joining us. I arrived at her place expecting her to welcome me with a warm hug. I had missed her. Instead, I was greeted with news of her friends who wanted a 'taste of me.'

"'Joining us to do what?' I asked, shocked at her statement. *Was I no longer her baby?* I thought to myself. Fear snaked up my throat like a boa constrictor, tightening its body around my throat. 'They want a taste of your tongue and your pussy,' she announced. It was no big deal for her. Her friends came—one chubby lady and a thin one. They were nice to me. Fear ran riot inside me when they entered the room. But aunty assured me I would be fine. And I was. They were gentle, and we all had a good time. Two of them joined us three more times, then they stopped coming. It was the turn of another set."

Ibinabo paused to catch her breath. I noticed her voice was hoarse. Jack sniffled. He was fighting back tears. My eyes were leaking already. I didn't have to think about it. The things she had to go through.

"'Why are these people here?' I asked Aunty when we were outside," Ibinabo continued with tears now flowing freely.

"I had excused myself from the room when both ladies entered the room. Aunty joined me outside. 'They want to fuck. What sort of question is that?'

"'Fuck who?' I asked aunty. I could not wrap my head around what she was saying. 'Are we changing them now? Is that what we are doing? Fucking all the girls in your compound? Fucking all your friends?' I was raising my voice now. I didn't mean to. The anger inside me was burning me. I could not control it," Ibinabo said.

"So all of you are lesbians? Is… Argh! I am not doing again o. I am tired. I am going to my house." I was mad at her.

"'This one you dey talk na rubbish.' Aunty's voice changed. It was heavier now. Serious. Unfriendly. She wasn't smiling now. It dawned on me now that we were talking business, and she was not going to watch me ruin it for her.

"'These girls have had their eyes on you since the first day they saw you. And it's not as if they are doing it for free. They have paid for their time, premium package o. So you better get yourself together. Let us go in there and do our job.' Aunty said without skipping a beat.

"Her interest in me was prurient from the start. The thought hit me like a Cristiano Ronaldo outside-the-box-eighteen riffle. I melted into nothingness, faded into darkness at the thought of it all. I fiddled with a strand of braid, wringing it around my pinky finger. *This was it*, I thought. *I was a lesbian prostitute, and I was still thirteen. I am still a child!* The thought struck a deadly blow inside me, so deadly I started crying. I didn't think of crying, didn't want to cry. It just happened."

Again, Ibinabo paused to let the words sink in. The fan stopped. The clock ticked in slow motion. Time stopped as we all waited for her. The pain had spread in the room like a virus. We were affected, and we couldn't help it. We were all sobbing. I cleaned the tears on my face with the hem of my shirt. It was Jack's Barcelona jersey. Jack shifted in his seat. He was trying to form macho, but his emotions were getting the best of him. The emotions were winning. Meanwhile, Ibinabo smiled weakly at us.

"She and her friends had already stripped naked when I entered," Ibinabo continued talking. Her shirt was off again.

"For the first time since I knew aunty, I saw female flesh, bare and unashamed, and I felt the wave of shame wash over me. I was a whore, and I was disgusting, and I was a piece of poor trash, and I was worthless. Breasts, the very item that drew the attention of aunty, seeing that same breasts on the chest of these women made me wish I were male. Breast is evil. Breast is a gift from the devil. Cut it off, Ibinabo. Cut the damn thing off and be free!"

I nodded in agreement. I didn't understand what she meant when she said breast was evil, but I knew what feeling like a waste was. I felt like that almost every day. In that moment, as stupid as it was, I wished I knew who my mother was. I wished I had somebody I could call mommy.

"I had no option," Ibinabo said. "My mind didn't want it, but my body did. I was in intense pain just seeing naked flesh and doing nothing. I dawdled at first, my mind drawing me back from grabbing the body of the slimmer one and ramming my tongue between her well-shaved thighs. But my body had a mind of its own. I yielded to its demands. And theirs." I shifted. The description was vivid. She was letting it all out now. No holds barred.

"They tied me to the bed midway into the kissing and analingus. I was surprised at first, but aunty assured me I'd be fine. She called it BDSM. I swear, the things they did to me that day: the whip; the slapping; the high stilettos they used to step on me; the dildo, bigger than anything I had ever seen; and the curse words that filled the room. It was loud, orgy, and bloody too. After the ordeal, *aunty* gave me thirty thousand naira. Aunty knew money was my magnet now. She knew the thing I had for her, if you called it love—although this love was misplaced and misunderstood, it was love at that time—you wouldn't be wrong, was dead. Fucking her, she realized now, was strictly business for me." Hearing Ibinabo use the *fuck* word so freely was weird. I also liked it, secretly.

"I didn't want to return, but Mama would not let me be. She kept asking me if I wouldn't go to aunty's place again. The bruises on my body did not bother her. All she wanted was the money. I guess she feared she might lose her mind if I told her the origin of the bruises. She preferred staying willfully ignorant, allowing her assumptions to be the only truth she held on to, instead of the truth."

Jack raised his hands as if about to ask a question in class. He asked Ibinabo if she hated her mother during that period. I, too, wanted to ask the same question.

"I did not really hate her," she replied.

"I returned two weeks later without so much a word of rebuke from Aunty," Ibinabo continued. "Two other ladies joined us this time. It was BDSM again, this time rougher and more painful. I endured it all, took in all the whipping, and even faked some moans and cries. If this was business, I figured, then I had to do it well. My envelope was bigger than the last time, but inside, I felt weak, small, and incognito.

"I told aunty I might not be coming again. She said it was fine by her. It was okay if I chose not to come, she said without any emotions. But I was the best in the game, she continued. And if I stayed long enough, rich women from PH, wives of politicians, women of power in the society would start looking for me. Listening to her was painful. Seeing that I was fast becoming a lesbian harlot at such a young age made me realize just how wrecked my life was."

"How were you able to deal with the pain?" Jack asked Ibinabo.

She did not respond. She continued with her story. The tears were still flowing freely. It was 11 p.m. Darkness enveloped the room as it did our aching hearts and teary eyes.

"Word was going around that I was the newest thing in the lesbian circle," Ibinabo said, "a girl genius. I only had to stay with her, allow her to guide me, and I'll be raking in the millions before I turned twenty.

"The offer was tempting, but I couldn't allow myself to become that kind of person. I thanked her and left. Three weeks at home without leaving the house to aunty's opened the faucet of Mama's curses and tongue lashing. She called me a useless girl who didn't want to help her poor mother. She insulted me, told me all sorts of things, just because I refused to sell my body to other women." Ibianbo was sobbing now. She could not hold back the tears anymore. I joined her sobbing. Jack was the man, so he tried consoling us by wrapping one arm around both of us.

"I kept mute. I knew telling her the truth would not change much," Ibinabo said after she caught her breath. Jack's hands were still on my shoulder.

"I wanted her to stay sane. I couldn't allow my mother to slip into depression. I could not allow Mama to go mad. I endured Mama for the next one year, choosing instead to sell things for people at the main market. Yes, a few times, I found myself needing money desperately. It was tempting—I'll be honest—to call aunty and get a quick gig with some of her friends, but I decided against it. I missed their bodies and the money and the thrill and all, but I had made up my mind not to go back to her. Boys around, young boys, became my go-to fixes. They didn't give me enough money—most were as broke as Wall Street—but I was foolishly certain I was in charge. I was not a prostitute, but I slept with a few guys for quick fixes. And I realized I liked men the same way I liked aunty and her friend."

Fear of Becoming Nothing

....

Ibinabo's gripping story made clearer the reason for her strong heart-edness. She was here, in my father's house, to survive. Survival was more important than rights and wrongs, more important than what a body deserved. For her, her body was no longer hers. She had lost it a long time ago. She walked around every day with each grain of clay cum flesh dropping away slowly. She was not Ibinabo, the girl with an amazing body. She was just Ibinabo. She was *just* another girl. The way she accepted her *justness,* her ordinariness, was frightening. Nothing can hurt a whiff of smoke. Ibinabo was a whiff of smoke draped with flesh. She was *nothing*. And I feared for what nothing would make me become.

Jack went back to his father, leaving *nothing* and I in the house. Like they say, when a man has given up on who he is, tomorrow is no longer a dream worth waiting for. It is a nightmare to be endured. Another painful part of time's fruitless journey one must live through.

Another thing Ibinabo's story did for me was question my unseen mother. I wondered what I would have done if my mother had not left me and eloped to some place. Although Ibinabo's mother wasn't the best of mothers, I still secretly wished mine was around. I had questions that no human could answer, or no human was ready to answer.

I told Ibinabo how I was feeling. She told me not to feel bad. She advised I should ask my dad about my mother's whereabouts.

I told her, "Dad would not answer me. He would not even listen to me."

"Then you should ask your grandmother. She should be able to give you the answers you need," Ibinabo said.

"Let me ask Jack what he thinks."

"All right then, you can. Jack would tell you the same thing I told you."

I asked for Jack's opinion in the evening of the same day. He agreed with Ibinabo's advice. The problem, however, I told them when we were in the room getting ready to retire to bed, was that I had no way to reach Grandma.

"Aunty Siya used to give me her phone to talk to Grandma when she was around. But I can't ask Aunty Damaris. She would just eat me up before I finish talking."

"I can help you with that one then," Ibinabo replied.

"I will find a phone for you tomorrow."

"How is that even possible? You don't have a phone, do you?" Jack asked with concern. Jack and I knew Ibinabo was older and was able to do certain things that we couldn't, yet we feared she might do something irrational one day. Her subtle show of defiance after the beating was something to worry over. But the fresh brightness in her eyes—one that didn't speak of love or happiness but a willingness to defy the odds, break the rules—was frightening.

"I would be going to the hospital with Aunty Damaris tomorrow morning. I know where I can get a phone for you."

"I am not sure I understand what you just said," I interjected.

"You don't have to understand. Just get ready to call your grandma tomorrow. I will make a phone available in the evening."

Aunty Damaris was heavy with a child during this period. Dad gave her money to prepare fried rice and chicken for us that day. He didn't say why we were having fried rice when it was not Christmas, neither did Aunty Damaris. But Ibinabo knew. She overheard Aunty Damaris, according to Ibinabo, telling one of her friends through WhatsApp voice notes about her pregnancy. From the conversation Ibinabo heard, Aunty Damaris was to tell Dad about the sex of the child before the end of the week.

"But how do you know the pregnancy is the reason for this cele-bration?" Jack asked. We were in the living room slicing the cabbage. Aunty Damaris went outside to answer her call.

"Because there is no way Aunty Damaris would go through this stress for nothing. Dad gave her enough money for the food; more-over, can't you see how giddy she is? Does this woman ever show kindness except it favors her?" Ibinabo reasoned. She was doing the slicing of the cabbage while I sliced the carrot.

"So how far gone do you think she is now, aunty doctor?" Jack asked jokingly.

"I don't know o, but e suppose don go far sha."

I listened as Jack and Ibinabo gave names to the unborn child, vividly describing how he would look, how wicked he would be, and even how he would sound like his mother.

"How do you know it is going to be a boy?" I asked. Somehow, we believed Ibinabo's story of Aunty Damaris gender reveal.

"She is looking more beautiful than before, haven't you guys noticed it?" Ibinabo asked.

"Yes, I think she looks a lot more finer," Jack answered.

Being Aunty Damaris's handbag on her antenatal visits became Ibinabo's additional chore. She didn't complain because, according to her, she gets to have a few minutes to herself while Aunty Damaris waited in the long queue for her turn. Aunty Damaris used the gen-eral hospital instead of a private hospital. General hospitals were bet-ter for pregnant women, Aunty Damaris told dad. They also had a rich thriving community of pregnant women. He had returned to find her tired. He complained about her not going to the private hospital he registered her in.

Ibinabo returned home in the afternoon with a wide smile. Aunty Damaris had gone to her store while Ibinado came home.

"Take," she gave me a small Nokia phone. "Call your grandma. There is enough airtime for you. Be fast. The boy said I should return the phone in the next one hour."

I collected the phone, too happy to say thank you. I collected a paper from my pocket. I had gotten my grandma's number from my dad's phone. I dialed the number. It rang five times, no answer.

I dialed again. It rang five times. No answer. Grandma was probably outside doing something while her phone was inside the house. She was fond of staying far away from her phone. I dialed again. After the third ring, I heard Grandma's velvety voice.

"Grandma, it is me, Belema." I was more happy than tense hearing her voice. I never knew I missed Grandma that much.

"Belema, which phone is this one you are using to call me?"

"Grandma, it is—"

"Belema, how are you? How is your father and his wife? We have missed you o. Your grandfather and I were even planning on coming to see you. Your father doesn't even call as often since he married that woman. My daughter, how is his wife treating you? Are you eating well? I heard she is pregnant, ehn, Belema is that true—"

Grandma kept on like that for the next minute. The happiness in her voice was evident in her rapid talk. She said she missed me so much, she was even thinking I should spend the holiday with her. I somehow managed to answer all the questions. I didn't have enough time to be answering plenty questions.

When she was satisfied with her questioning, she inquired again where I had gotten the phone I was using. She knew the phone wasn't my dad's, she told me.

"Na Ibinado give me the phone. Please, Granny, no more questions. I wanted to ask you a question. It is very important."

"Okay. Belema, what is wrong? This one you want to ask me important question. What is the matter?"

"Grandma, it is nothing serious."

"Okay, I am all ears," Grandma said. Her voice took on the serious tone. I felt it, and I could not say the words. I was the only one in the room as Jack and Ibinabo left me to talk to Grandma alone. The weather was hot. The sun was out in full force. Afternoons were usually exceedingly hot in August. The weather had melted my initial confidence.

"Uhm, Grandma," I managed to start after seconds of silence. "Grandma, can you hear me?" I asked. Grandma was quiet too. I knew she was still on the line. I was looking for an excuse to end the call.

"Belema, I am here. What is the question you want to ask me?"

"Uhm, Grandma, please don't be angry at this question o." I was afraid. I didn't want Grandma to get angry at me. I don't want her to think I was ungrateful for all she and Grandpa did for me.

"Granny," I continued, "you know I am a big girl now." I said the big girl to help ease the tension. She giggled.

"I know you are."

"I am almost eleven now, and, Granny, I feel lost sometimes." I didn't know where the word *lost* came from, but it was true, talking to Granny that afternoon. I was able to give name to the pain I had been feeling.

"Belema, lost? How? Aren't you at home?" Concerned Grandma.

"I am at home. I feel like my life is not with me. It is as if I am another person. Granny," the courage was coming now. I needed to let the words out of my mouth before fear stole it from me.

"Belema, I am listening to you. What is making you feel lost?"

"Where is my mother? Why did she leave me? Why did she not take me with her when she was leaving? Where is she now? Why didn't she ever come back for me all this time? Is she dead? What does she even look like? Why did I not see any of her picture?" I rattled on. The words had finally come out. The tightness in my chest when I collected the phone to call Grandma loosened significantly. Although Grandma's silence was making me wish I hadn't asked the question, yet I felt good. I felt free. *Whatever answer Granny gave me, I was prepared*, I thought to myself.

"Belema," Grandma's voice, somber and somewhat broken, called from the other end of the call. "I understand what you are feeling. And I am sorry for any pain or anger you are feeling." Her voice was breaking. Sobs escaped her. She was crying.

"I would answer your questions when I come to visit you. And I would be coming soon. My daughter, I am sorry for any pain you are feeling. Your mother loves you. She does." Sobs. More sobs. I listened, trying my best not to cry. Beads of sweat pouring out of my skin had nothing on the ache I was feeling. My heart was stretching itself, asking me if I could take it. I couldn't. I broke down in tears listening to my grandmother cry. We both cried on the phone for a minute. Crying with my grandmother, over the phone, was a great release for me. She promised to come to visit so she could explain everything to me.

But like everything in my life, nothing ever worked. Nothing. Grandma did not come.

The Last Straw Must not Be Drawn, You Take It out Yourself

Dad's discipline "wickedness and cruelty" aged like fine wine. The older he got, the more he watched us like bald eagles watch their eaglets. He was not relenting on the type of punishment he meted out to Ibinabo and I.

Five years went by with the cruelty of my father and the nonchalance of my stepmother growing in proportion. In those five years, one would have thought they would treat us differently, but they instead raised the bar. Ibinabo and I got used to the treatment the same way a virus gets used to an antidote, masking the qualities. *The cane*, both of us thought, *was losing its sting*. We had mastered the art of getting beat. But we lied.

Aunty Damaris, in the four-year span, had given birth to two handsome children. She cherished them like treasures. And they were treasures. Damian and David were the most caring kids I had ever met.

The day Damian was brought to the house from the hospital, his two-year-old brother, David could not get enough of him. David stayed by his side all day long for one week. Even when the maid Aunty Amara and Aunty Damaris's friend had tried to take him away, the poor boy wouldn't leave. He bawled his eyes out when Ibinabo begged him to leave the baby so the mother could bathe him. He was such a sweetheart.

He was one of the reasons why my hatred for Aunty Damaris melted into indifference. She was like a ghost to me. Nothing she did mattered. Since Grandma's shocking sickness that stopped her from coming four years ago, and my father's refusal to allow me to visit Grandma (which was greatly influenced by Aunty Damaris), my hate for her got to its peak. But Damian's birth and his sweet nature made me forgive her. At least she was here for her children. My mother could not stay.

Ibinabo didn't seem to mind the treatment. She grew fond of Damian and the house help. The help, a woman in her midfifties, acted like a mother to Ibinabo. The help wasn't all caring, loving, and mushy. None of that. But she talked to Ibinabo a few times. She was always giving Ibinabo motherly advice. Although Ibinabo didn't particularly trust her, saying to me on many nights that the help was a fraud. Still, Ibinabo listened to the woman's wisdom.

It was the help that encouraged Ibinabo to look for handwork to do. According to her, being a fine girl was not all that mattered anymore. She needed to have a handwork, the woman advised, else she'd be a liability in her husband's house. Ibinabo hated the words "husband's house."

Ibinabo grew to become more beautiful, more rebellious in a silent way, the type of rebellion one could not overtly place a finger on but could tell from the testy response she gave when asked questions. She was getting older, but Dad would not recognize it. As long as she was in his house, he would brag she was under his care and discipline. He was not going to allow any of his daughters—Ibinabo and I—to become wayward. He found a place for Ibinabo to learn fashion designing after his proposal to send her to a polytechnic was met with stern criticism by his wife. She argued that Ibinabo needed to learn something that would help her make money fast so she could help her mother. Her argument, on the surface, sounded reasonable, but we knew better. Ibinabo was grateful for the opportunity to leave the house every day.

She was learning fast. Her dedication and knack for fashion design was incredible. Within three months of attending the fashion school, she started drawing design sketches. She used her Android phone (I was surprised Dad did not seize it from her after he caught her watching lesbian porn. Her attitude shooed him away.) to watch videos on YouTube.

"I want to learn this fashion designing so that I can help my siblings. They need to go to school. I need them to be educated, to have a better shot at life." Her wisdom never stopped wowing me. I listened to her talk about her day at work: the clothes they sewed, the designs she and her fellow apprentices drew, the wickedness of her madam, and the way guys were flocking into their shop to sew clothes. She reeled me with many stories of her sexual escapades as well.

"I don't want you to be like me, ignorant of what sex is. I can't say what I am doing, the things I am telling you, I can't say this is sex education, but this is the best I can do for now. I am teaching you what I know and how I know it."

She taught me about menstruation before I saw my first blood. I was in JSS3 when it happened. I had returned from school exhausted. I washed my uniform and Dad's clothes in the washing machine. I cooked white rice. There was stew in the fridge. I dished Aunty Damaris and Ibinabo's food in their food flask. I delivered the food to them and returned home to rest. The plan was for me to take a nap before waking to do my assignment, but I was fagged out. I overslept. Ibinabo returned early from the shop to meet me sleeping. She didn't disturb me, figured I was tired after a stressful day at school. I woke around 7 p.m. to find a pool of blood on the bed. At first, I thought I imagined it. When I cleared my eyes and saw it was real, panic took over.

What was wrong with me? Why am I bleeding? What did I do today to deserve this bleeding?

I knew this was menstruation, but I was still scared, questioning why it had to happen that day. *I didn't do anything bad today in school*, I thought. I didn't even kiss my boyfriend, so why this? I was still sitting on my bed, confused as a crossword puzzle when Ibinabo entered the room. Seeing her gave me the cold-water relief a thirsty desert traveler gets when he finally tastes the chill of water. My body relaxed immediately. She would know what to do.

She saw me sitting still. "What is the problem?" her eyes were asking. I pointed to the bed.

"Wetin happen for—"

She understood. She didn't laugh at me, at my fear. She didn't make it feel weird, or as if it was something to be ashamed of. She smiled at me, sat down close to me, and took my hands into hers.

"You should not be afraid of this." She looked at the bed. "This is what makes you a woman. It is your rite of passage into womanhood. And never you be ashamed of it either. There is nothing disgraceful about your period. We have talked about this before, am I right?"

I nodded.

"Good. So as we've discussed, do the needful, and you will be fine. Do you still have the set of sanitary pads I gave you?"

"Yes, I do. They are in the wardrobe."

"Good. Clean up and use them. Belema, remember, this is a big deal, and it also isn't. It all depends on how you handle it. Don't be afraid of your blood, never be. This thing you are ashamed of, it is yours and yours alone. Nobody should make you feel inferior because of this monthly blood ritual. Do you hear me?"

"I do. I will be confident in my body, always assured of who I am and what my body represents," I said, mouthing off the *body* affirmations she taught me.

"Beautiful. I will help you wash the bedspread. Take it off, wash up, and use the pad. You are fine. You hear?"

She was so sweet and caring, I often wondered why she had to live in a dungeon like my house. I wondered why God didn't make this right and easy for a human as loving as Ibinabo.

Dad did not stop beating Ibinabo whenever he felt she was out of line. She was nineteen, all grown up and looking like a woman, but Dad still shouted at her on the days she came home later than 8 p.m.

On one of such days, Ibinabo had gone out on a date with her boyfriend. She told me she would be coming home late, so I should help her do the dishes.

"What would you do when Dad asks after you, and I tell him, or Aunty Damaris tells him you are not around? How would you deal with his shouting and his madness?" I was spreading the bedspread for us to sleep. I was in SS2, preparing for my senior West African Examinations Council exams. The exam was a dreaded one as it was always tough for students to scale through even for students in SS3; nevertheless, I knew I had the grades to deliver a good result.

"I don't care what he does. I am used to his shouting and madness and beating. E no dey affect me again," she replied. She took off her shirt and slid out of her trouser. There was power, but she liked sleeping with her bra and panties.

"You sure say that man never don go look for new ways to take punish us? The other day I see am dey watch video for YouTube," I joked before arranging the pillows at the head of the bed.

"E fit be o. If you collect his Samsung S7 and check his YouTube search history, I am certain you would see searches like new ways to kill children in the name of punishment."

We both laughed. I believed Dad was researching new ways to discipline us (read kill us before our time). He had tried all the punishment methods in the book: beating with cane, koboko, electric wire. He had hurled all the throwable items at us. He had used pepper and water, used razor blade and pepper, and used hot water and hot iron and public walk of shame. Dad had practically tried every form of punishment in the thick big *book of punishment masked as discipline.*

Dad asked Aunty Damaris why Ibinabo hadn't returned home by eight. Aunty Damaris, clueless, told Dad that there was something holding her back at work. "It was normal sometimes for ogas to hold an apprentice back if they had lots of work to do," she explained. I was perplexed she could come up with something that truthful. Whether she was trying to defend Ibinabo by saying what she said, or she said it with all the innocence in the world, I would not know, but it cooled the situation a bit. We ate dinner: Banga soup and eba. I cleared the table, washed the plates, and swept the kitchen. It was as I was mopping the kitchen Dad asked again why Ibinabo hadn't come home.

"Which kind of work was she doing that she can't call to inform anybody? Does she know what the time is?"

"I would call her oga now to ask her why she hadn't returned," Aunty Damaris replied. She was uncharacteristically supportive of Ibinabo that night. It was strange.

She returned to the living room minutes later to tell Dad that Ibinabo's oga had closed since 6 p.m. The oga told her that Ibinabo even left work early to do some things at home.

Here was my cue to tell Dad what was happening. Dad was pissed at the new information. Where in hell's name did Ibinabo go to?

"Dad," my trembling voice began, "she went out with her boyfriend. She said if you asked that I should tell you she went on a date with her—"

The metallic hand of my father's landed on my face. It ruffled my cheekbones. Cracked? Maybe a little.

"She went out with her what? Her boyfriend? In my house?"

"But, Dad, she is no longer a baby. She has a right to—"

Another whack across the face. Then another. My father was pissed beyond what his bladder could hold. Unleash-the-beast mode. The mention of *boyfriend* sparked something inside my dad, something that resembled familiarity. Like he knew something he wasn't telling us, some secret.

"Do you have that stupid boyfriend's number?" he asked.

"I don't have it," I replied. My voice trembled and my teeth clattered like broken plates.

He got up from the sofa, went into his room, came out with a rope, and sat back on the sofa. Aunty Damaris sat at one corner of the living room, silent as a lamb. But I read fear in her eyes. Was she genuinely scared for Ibinabo? Was she trembling inside her because of Ibinabo? This is strange. Something was not right.

For the next twenty minutes, we all waited in the living room for Ibinabo: me counting the number of tiles in the parlor and the ones with stains on them; Aunty Damaris wearing the most concerned look I had ever seen on her; and Dad standing, sitting, walking, pulling his shirt, and getting koboko from his room. Walking, standing, and sitting again, he was a restless mess.

At exactly 9:57 p.m., Ibinabo knocked. I went to open the door for her. At the door, I told her she was in deep shit. She smiled and told me not to worry. She hugged me and whispered she got something for me. It was outside, in a nylon bag. I should get it later at night when my parents were sleeping. She had changed into her work clothes.

"Good evening, sir. Good evening, Ma. Good evening, Mama Amara," she greeted Dad and Aunty Damaris and our maid.

"Ibinabo, what is the time? Why are you coming back home now?" was Dad's reply.

Ibinabo didn't say anything. She stood like a statue, looking at Dad as his anger became a whirlwind. She was prepared for whatever would happen. Mama Amara stared at her like she was a ghost. She looked like her eyes would fall off. Her jaw dropped. She was surprised.

"So you don't have mouth to talk again, abi? Don't you have a mouth? You think you are grown, abi, mature? You think you can do anything you like in my house—"

Ibinabo pulled off her top, revealing a bare chest. She slipped out of her black jeans. She was bare, too, down there. She came prepared. She produced a nylon filled with Cameroon pepper from her handbag.

"Daddy, here, I have the pepper. You don't have to send Aunty Damaris or Mama Amara to get it. I have what you need."

She dropped the pepper on the ground, went closer to him, her breast bouncing as she walked. Looking at her from behind, it was obvious Ibinabo was a grown woman, and beating her was inhumane and wicked. I hoped beyond hope that Dad would resist the urge to fall for this. Her attitude was defiant, and to be frank, I loved it. *Only if Dad would not fall for the bait*, I thought. She needed something to crack, something to break so she could leave. She had complained to me several times that she was tired of his treatment and how he made us look like slaves. She needed something to trigger it. I knew it deep down.

The nylon at my dad's feet, Ibinabo lay on the ground. Dad was angry. Hell, *enraged* is not the right word for how intense his anger was. Such effrontery! He must have exclaimed in his mind.

He did the usual: took the rope, tied her hands and legs, applied pepper mixed with water all over her body and in her private part, and flogged her with Koboko. As he was tying her hand, Aunty Amara pleaded with my dad to forgive Ibinabo. She thought her voice mattered. She knew it didn't. Still, she begged him to take it easy. Dad never listens when he was angry.

He added electric wire to the mix. As he flogged, his anger devouring him, Ibinabo didn't make a single sound. She didn't cry when Dad applied the pepper to her vagina, didn't shake when he started flogging her, and didn't turn as he struck her with his weapon of child correction. The defiance was premium content. Dad, enraged as a diseased horse, kept hitting her. The more she stayed still, the angrier he got, and with each threshold of anger he reached, he raised his arm higher, his blow struck more, and the koboko licked more skin and drew more blood. But Ibinabo was not shaking.

I wanted to beg her to cry, to roll, to do anything, to move her damn muscle before my dad killed her in the fit of his anger. She was not going to allow him to win this. She remained still on the ground. Whatever she was trying to do was not working on my father. Her flesh was tearing so fast, I feared she would be left with bones by the time he finished. He was annoyed that Ibinabo wasn't responding, so he got one of our dog chains, put it on her neck, and started pulling her to the streets as usual. Aunty Damaris, like me, was standing, unable to do anything. She was crying, sobbing so silently. I saw in her eyes that day, for the first time, pity for a human that wasn't her. I couldn't believe my eyes.

"Honey, please, leave her," she said between sobs. She stopped Dad's raised arm from hitting Ibinabo again. His koboko hit her instead. She held on to his hand, suspended in the air, and begged him to drop the koboko. She led him to their room, all the while crying. Aunty Amara sat there, bewildered, or was she numb? Her jaw was still dropped, and her hand tried holding them together. The hands failed woefully.

I woke the next morning, after I had taken Ibinabo in, washed her up, and gave her pain relief, to find a note inside my Bible. She was out of our house for good. *She was tired of it all,* her letter read. Her handwriting, I noticed, wasn't as beautiful as her. *She was going to stay with friends, and I should not tell anybody where she was.* She would write to me as often as she could. She was not going back to her madam's shop again. She had learned enough and would see how she would survive alone. As I read the letter, hot tears poured from my face. The tiny part of me still left had been taken away. Ibinabo took the last strand of joy from me. She was the only reason I could endure my father's punishment. Now she was gone, I was dead inside.

alone again

....

Some people help define who and what we are. These people, it might seem at the start, are regular humans, and we sometimes underestimate their importance because of familiarity. But when the tide of time shifts their tectonic plates to some other place, we feel the canyon they once filled widen. We slip into ourselves, hoping to fill the space they left. Sometimes, for those who are late to the realization, we pretend we don't miss them, that we don't need them. We tell ourselves we can live without them. We have always lived without them. We argue with our emotions, so why can't we continue living without them.

It was three days after Ibinabo left that I learned the true story behind Grandma's manufactured sickness. A woman from the village came to deliver a message to Dad. The men in the family were to contribute money for the burial of an older family member. The woman, a messenger from the council of elders in the village, was sent to meet family members in Lagos. Dad was aware of the woman's visit. What he wasn't aware of, however, was the message the "other" message the woman was sent to deliver. Grandma sent her.

The woman was a member of Dad's extended family who lived not too far from us. She was assigned to collect monies from members in the city. On the day she came to the house, Aunty Damaris was away at her store, the help was busy in the kitchen, and my half-brothers were running around the house. I welcomed her and gave her a cup of chilled water. She had visited us before in the past, not sure why though. While the help was preparing a small something for her, I stayed with her in the living room. It was rude to leave a visitor alone there. Somebody must keep the visitor's company. I was making small talk, asking about her children and business when she shushed me. I was waiting for the small something, which is well-prepared food with big chunks of meat, to come before running to my room. Ibinabo's disappearance was still fresh.

The woman, after gulping down the second glass of chilled water, told me my grandmother sent her to me. Her face had a few wrinkles that looked like they were tired of living on her face. She wore a bright smile Jack would have called fake. It was too bright. She brought out a brown envelope from her old dusty black handbag. She handed the letter to me and whispered that I should keep it away from Dad. That nobody should know about the letter. I collected the envelope and hid it under my blouse before the maid came in. Dad returned twenty minutes later, and she delivered her second message.

According to the letter Grandma sent (which was detailed, I guess Grandpa helped her with the writing.), she didn't come to the house because my father had warned her not to. According to the letter, when she called my dad to tell him about my call, Dad was furious. He felt I was ungrateful. He said he never stopped my mother from visiting, and if she cared so much, she would have come looking for me and not the other way round. Granny wrote that she could do nothing about it as Papa warned her to stay out of my father's business.

Dad also felt that Granny staying away from me for a long time was a good option. He believes she made his work tougher. He said I was a spoiled brat. The longer Grandma was away, the faster I forgot about my mom. And if I forgot about my mom, it means I won't ask Granny more questions. Even though Grandma felt the judgment was unfair on her and me, she understood my dad's anger and protection.

But she was tired of keeping mute about my mother, she wrote in the letter. She told me that she had an inkling that maybe my mother was married to someone else now, and she probably didn't disclose her past to this person. She had given herself a fresh start, and I was not in that new chapter of her life. She did not know my mom's exact location. So she told me that I needed to keep praying for her to return and things to get better. With all that Grandma wrote in the letter, it was clear being a mother was too much for her. She needed a break. The letter, and Ibinabo leaving, was too much trauma for me to handle. I lied to myself that Ibinabo leaving was a piddling action that would have nothing on me. But each day brought me closer to harmattan. My heart grew cold. My reluctance to dance to my father's music increased. My rebellion was not visible, neither was it subtle. It happened in my head. I defied my father in my thoughts, refusing to pander to his obsolete method of parenting and discipline. I would, in my head, tell him to his face that he was a wicked devil-faced bastard who should be burning in the deepest parts of hell. I would raise my hand to stop his incoming koboko strike, suspending the hand in the air before storming out of his presence. He would stand, mouth agape, and watch me walk out on him. He wouldn't be able to say anything. She's grown wings. He would later tell his wife. She has grown wings. I would go out whenever I liked, returned when I felt like it, and he would say nothing. He'd sigh and tell me the fly that refuses to listen to the words of the elders would, I would complete his wacky proverb with "only if that fly hasn't been living in the mortuary all the while." And I pictured, in my head, that I'd stand akimbo, chewing my gum, blowing gum bubbles to his face before flicking my hair, and then I'd walk out again. In all my disrespectful scenes, I always stormed out. In all the internal turmoil, I let some pain out by talking to Aunty Amara. Seeing she was fond of Ibinabo, I thought she was the only person who would understand my predicament. And she did. Or I thought she did. She told me that I would be fine. That she, too, missed Ibinabo. Her presence was a kind of buffer for me. But it didn't help much. I was alone, and no amount of you-will-be-fine talk could fill the lacuna in my heart.

One month after the heart-shrinking pain, walking out was what I truly wanted to do, but I was too scared to walk out. I stayed back because where could I go? My mother was a forgotten chapter in my life. Calling her a chapter even makes it seem as if she was featured in any way in my life. I never saw her. I never heard from her. I didn't know what she looked like. I could be with her in a club, dancing with her, and I wouldn't know it was her. I could even be with her in a cab and pay my fare, and I would not know she was the one. She was not a chapter, just an idea, a dead idea I never wanted to remember. I was stuck in my father's house.

I woke one morning, struck by the slithering demon called depression. I was lying on the bed, resigned not to go to school. It was a Thursday, sports day in school, and we were expected to do some random exercises. I wasn't ready to do any of that shit. Aunty Damaris took her two sons: David and Damian to school. David was four years old while Damian was two years old. The maid had traveled to her village in Ebonyi State to take care of her sick mother. Aunty Damaris asked me if I'd be going to school. I told her I would. Explaining depression to a woman like her was like pouring water in a desert. She might even beat me for feeling depressed.

When she was out of the house, I searched the medicine nylon in my dad's room for pills. I found some random medicine in the nylon. Death was a better escape from all this madness. I poured several of the tablets on the table in my room, got a bottle of water from the fridge, and a plastic cup from the kitchen. I knew taking my life wasn't going to be easy, but it was way easier to die than to live in this house. I would run away from here, and it would be final. I took the drugs and waited for them to kill me. I knew nobody would be coming home. I would die, and nobody would shed a tear. The drugs didn't work until three hours later. I was tired of waiting for the drug's effect to kick in, so I slept. I would slink away into the other side of the world unconscious. I was dreaming of Dakumo and the wristband she gave me, fiddling with it, talking to her through the wristband.

I knew she could hear me. I was telling her I was tired of staying in this place. I told her the plans we had, plans of toys and dolls and fine things I would bring for her in the village were all going south now. "I wished I never left the village," I said to the invisible Dakumo. I wished she would see me, broken and tired. I told Dakumo I was going to the other place because this one was too painful for me. She didn't respond. She wasn't there. But a strong gust of wind blew me away from the dream and blew me back to reality. My stomach was rumbling with a sharp knife-splitting kind of pain when I awoke from the dream. *It was happening*, I thought. I was dying now. In no time, I would be free from this place.

Escape was finally coming to fruition. I closed my eyes. The pain kept tearing the insides of my stomach, slicing it open like a suya man working on a piece of suya. "*I will not shout*," I assured myself. I didn't want to attract the attention of the empty house. I would die in silence. Hasn't silence been my only language since I came to this house? Didn't this house swallow my voice? Didn't it make me a shadow of my bubbly self, making me retract into an apology of a child? I was going to wear my silence to heaven.

But I couldn't help it. The pain was numbing. The pain dragged the words out of my mouth, overriding my mind's will to keep numb and die in silence. As I kept screaming, rolling on the floor of my room, thrashing about, hands flailing, legs kicking—all in a quest to release the crippling pain—I wished it would all end sooner.

Darkness approached me as I screamed on. I saw the face of darkness. It was gorgeous. I offered my arm to it—darkness—to lead me wherever it wanted to. I was its slave, a willing one, and I was ready to do its bidding, to follow it to whatever parts of hell, or heaven, it chose to lead me. Just when darkness's arm and mine touched, I heard the door slam. I wanted the darkness to clutch me and drag me off before any form of help came. But darkness was slow. It waited till Aunty Damaris barged into my room. It stood still as she cried for help from our neighbors. Darkness watched her go outside, cry for help, and return to my room with three guys. Darkness did nothing to take my outstretched arm when the men hauled me on their back and took me to the hospital.

I did not die. Darkness refused to grant me the escape I needed.

My recovery was fast. I spent one week in the hospital. I returned home, planning on other ways to escape. Dad didn't talk to me about my suicide attempt. He acted like what happened was the most normal thing in the world. Like I fell ill, and he took me to the hospital to get treated. The doctors who treated me didn't ask any questions. The silence in my house found its way to the hospital.

The other escape, after pills had failed me, was running away. Ibinabo had given me her address, and I knew I could run to her. But running to her would put her in more trouble, so I decided against it.

Just run, anywhere. You don't have to know where you are headed. Anywhere is better than this place.

My escape plan was still in the works when Ibinabo's mother visited us. She wanted her daughter. She told Dad after she finished the eba and vegetable soup Aunty Damaris served her. She looked like Ibinabo: tall, great shape with deep-set eyes, flat nose, silky hair that had strands of gray between them, and dry and parched skin. It has seen better days, that skin of hers. She thanked my father for all he had done. She wanted to see her daughter and take her to live with her since things were beginning to shape up for her.

Dad's cockiness could not take a break. He told Ibinabo's mother that in his attempt to discipline Ibinabo, she ran out of his house. He used the word "discipline" as if it were true. To him, he was only trying to "train up a child in the way she should go so that when she grows old, she will not depart from it." He was pretty sure what he was doing was right.

The information did not meet Ibinabo's mom well. She sat still, looking into space. Her hands were on her arms. Then tears started leaking, slowly at first, and then they gushed in their torrents. Dad said nothing and did nothing. Although he was responsible for Ibinabo, he said he wasn't the reason for her disappearance. He assured Ibinabo's mother she was fine wherever she was. After all, she had learned fashion designing. "She would be able to sustain herself with that," he told Ibinabo's mother. Confused about what to do next, she thanked Dad and Aunty Damaris, gathered her broken pieces, and stood up. She would take the bus and embark on the three-hour journey back to her house without her daughter. *Life was fair!*

I met Ibinabo's mother outside as she was headed for the bus park. Dad said he was too tired to drive her there. Instead, he gave her two thousand naira for her fare. Glancing over my shoulder, looking left and right to make sure my father wasn't anywhere close, I explained how she would get to Ibinabo's place. Ibinabo didn't want anybody to find her. She trusted me not to tell anybody. But seeing the pain in her mother's eyes, I explained to Ibinabo's mother that I was breaking a promise by telling her.

"Ibinabo go explain wetin really happen for our house."

I hurried out before my father saw me.

Each day became too dreadful for me. The beatings from my father, the hatred from my stepmother, and the loneliness I felt. I decided just to run away. Two months after Ibinabo's mother visited us, I scribbled a note. It read, "I am running away, and you people would never see me again." I chose a Saturday to run away. Since there was nowhere for me to run to, I figured wandering the road on a Saturday morning offered me better chances of not dying.

I thought of running to Grandma. She would accept me even though she had been warned never to tell me about my mother. But she did and that opened a can of bees that stung me all through the years since then. Thoughts of Grandma and that letter made me want to curse myself for being a demonic child. I had burnt that letter. I did not ever want Dad to see it and have another reason to hate Granny more. The knowledge that my father could never get to know about the letter was satisfactory to me.

Another thought occurred to me: Maybe I could go to my friend's house? I thought to go there. Her mum would care for me. But I would be causing the innocent woman trouble she didn't deserve. There was nowhere to run to. I settled for running to the streets.

I slipped the paper under a cup on the living room table and left the house when everybody was still sleeping. The time was 6:05 a.m. I wandered the streets I was familiar with for a while before venturing further into streets I had never seen. If I didn't see a river to jump into, I concluded, I would walk myself to total exhaustion and then die from fatigue. I passed streets with thatched roof and walls with washed-off paints. I passed a street where all the houses were mud.

The children on that street were only clad in pants that had seen their best days. The children, around two to three years old, sat comfortably on the ground, playing with sands. Some, like one boy with a bloated stomach, was taking a dump and munching on bread at the same time. I hadn't moved too far from this street when a car zoomed past me. The sun wasn't out yet.

"Get inside the car now!" was the voice that came from the car. The car stopped a few meters from where I stood. I knew what it meant: I am never escaping the hellhole. My father didn't have to come out of the car for me to do as I was told. I scuffled my feet, opened the door of the car, and entered. If what I did had a consequence, I didn't know. I didn't think so. But I knew, seeing the level of chill of my father, that there was going to be serious consequences for my action.

He drove off, deposited me in the house, and went to watch football. I said deposited because he didn't have to utter a word when we drove past the gate. I knew to leave the car, go to my room, and act like nothing happened. He returned at night and said absolutely nothing to me. I didn't feel anything. No pain! No regrets! Nothing. Aunty Damaris didn't bother asking me what had happened. She had sense enough to know the depth of trouble I was in. And I am sure she gloated inside at my predicament. My half-brothers didn't come to my room to play with me. My countenance the moment I walked through the door by 8 a.m. when Dad dropped me at home was icy as the North Pole. Dad's silence that night meant one thing: He was planning a disciplinary master class. I waited for it, hopeful it would end my misery and help me escape finally.

I Grew Out of My Skin

....

When winter has taken residence in your chest, the sun has to work extra hours to get a drip of liquid emotion flowing from you. I was rock-hard emotionally. I wasn't emotionally dead—I still felt some form of love for things—but I was at the precipice of an icy river. I could fall off any time. Dad decided that silence was the best punishment for me as well as grounding me to stay at home. He said since I could not be trusted when I was allowed to go out, then I had to stay locked up.

You see, he never bothered asking me why I tried to run. Or tried to kill myself. He never inquired why leaving his house was now my life's goal. He didn't care. He never did. His last punishment was the final straw that broke me.

I went to my classmate's house to discuss how we would turn up for our SS3 dinner. I was desperate to find happiness and be around people that could make me laugh, even if for a few minutes. When I reached her house, I met two other classmates there. The gist started with what we should wear for the dinner and then it morphed into boys and boyfriends and dinner dates. I was so caught up in the conversation, I forgot to watch the time. I checked my watch when the room was growing dark. 8:45 p.m. I was dead. I wanted to hurry back home so I could explain to Dad what had happened. *But on second thought*, I thought, *damn it! I'll enjoy my stay here. These other girls don't have two heads*. I left my friend's house by 9:30 p.m. I got home, and as was expected, Dad was waiting for me.

I wanted to do an Ibinabo, but Dad was prepared for me.

"Where are you coming from by this time of the night?" He was waiting for me in the living room. He switched off all the lights, except for a blue dim one.

"I went to my friend's place. I lost track of time."

I knew it changed nothing. Yet I answered. At his feet were a dog chain, a small bottle filled with pepper, and a bottle of water. His best friend—his koboko—was lying there, waiting to get to work. My Ibinabo spirit scuttled off to one corner when I saw the tools waiting for me.

"Strip!" he commanded.

I couldn't. I wouldn't do it. Not now. And not in a long time. I won't allow this man to make a mess of my body again. I kept still.

"Belema, I said take off all your clothes! Have you gone deaf?"

"Daddy, I am not taking them off. I am a grown girl. I only went out to see my friends, something you never allow me to do, and I lost track of time. Why should that be a big deal?" my croaky voice managed to say. Where the strength was coming from, I had no idea, but I was tired of silence. If I would die, at least let me die with my voice floating at my murder scene.

"I see you have grown wings. You are a big girl? Which kind of big girl? Because you have what? Or is it because you are almost done with secondary school, now that makes you feel you are grown?"

Because I am tired of your beatings, Dad. Because I am done giving my body to be tortured by you! Because I want to kill myself, but death doesn't want to take me. Because—The thoughts faded in my head. I started to cry. I took off my top and trousers. I was exhausted. After taking off my clothes with my bra and panties left, he glowered at me.

"Take those off too," he bellowed.

"I will not!"

He sprang to his feet, took three long strides toward me at the entrance of the living room, and grabbed my hand. I started kicking out, refusing to go with him. He was stronger than me. He dragged me to where he had been seating and pushed me down on the ground. I sat on the ground and watched him unfurl the dog chain. He tied my hand and legs with the chain. Then he slapped me on the face. I continued kicking out and fighting. He kept slapping me, telling me he would put the fear of God in me since I had lost it. Damian, obviously woken up by my cries, walked to his Dad. His eyes were sleepy.

"Daddy, stop beating sister Belema," little Damian begged.

His little hands tried to take the koboko from his father's. When he saw that his dad was not relenting in his slaps, he started to beat him. His tiny hands landed on the torso of his father. My father was so enraged that he shoved his two-year-old son with his hand, sending the kid tumbling. Damian yelped. His mother, who had been pretending all the while that she was sleeping, rushed out to carry her son.

"Since you think you have grown up and can fight me, you will sleep outside today."

I would be more than happy to sleep outside. He sprayed the water and pepper he mixed on my eyes. He beat me with the koboko so hard, I feared he would lose his arm. He dragged me outside with my bra and panties. It was a cold December night. I was locked outside the house under extreme cold with only a bra and panties. The experience sealed my fate: I was never going to stay here. I'd rather die than stayed here.

Two days of Dad and I avoiding each other like the plague, he came to my room to inform me I had been grounded. I was not to step out of the house till further notice. The dinner that led me here was one week away. I could not afford to miss it. Information from the grapevine had it that I would win a few awards, best in a few subjects. I did not object to his decree.

The importance of the dinner meant I could not miss it for anything in the world. So I thought I could trust Aunty Damaris and the maid to help me talk Dad out of the punishment.

"Aunty Damaris, please, I want you to help me beg Dad to allow me go for my school's graduation dinner. If you and Aunty Amara can help me beg him, I would be grateful. I would not go anywhere after this dinner. I promise you."

They both agreed to help me talk to Dad. Two days before D-Day, I sneaked out of the house, with help from Aunty Damaris, to the market. I bought the red gown and black heels I would be wearing to the dinner. The girls and I agreed on red gowns the last time I visited them—the day of my house arrest. I bought oranges and bananas for my brothers, facial cleanser for Aunty Damaris, and a loaf of bread for Aunty Amara, our maid. I gave them the little gifts I got for them, and they thanked me.

I was in my room that night, thinking of the things Karim told me at the market when I heard a knock on the door. Karim was a friend of Jack's at the gaming shop Jack used to visit. He reeled me on the sad tales of Jack's stepmother and dad. He told me how Jack suffered at the hands of the people he called parents. Jack's biological mother was dead. Karim said Jack, before he ran away from home, went through hell every day.

"The kind of things wey him own papa dey do am ehn, you sef go shock. You know how Jack dey form like say cain no dey enter him body? The one wey dem dey do am pass beating. Sometimes— this one no be person tell me, I see the mark for him body with my eyes—when dem send Jack message and him come back some few minutes late, him stepmother go cut under him leg, then she go put Cameroon pepper inside. The kind of marks Jack has on his body, the scars no be here. If you see Jack, you go cry for the boy."

I didn't know when tears started flowing from my eyes. I dropped the nylon bag containing my gown on the ground.

"How did he run away?" I wanted to know the strategy he used. I needed to know how he was able to run and where he ran to. I, too, needed to run. I needed an escape.

"One day o, the parents woke up and didn't see him in the house. He didn't leave any trace for them to use to find him. They didn't know most of his friends. The ones they knew, they threatened with police, but nothing came out of it. Jack has been missing for two years now. Nobody knows where he is, or if he's even still alive. And you know the funny thing"—Karim cleaned the beads of sweat with his handkerchief—"his father doesn't really care. The man is going about his normal life as if nothing happened. His second wife has children for him, so why should the man bother?"

Jack's story was both heart-wrenching and inspiring. It seemed like all three of us—Jack, Ibinabo, and I—had all tried to run. All but me have been successful in our escape plan. *After this dinner*, I thought, *I would finally make my escape final.*

The knock on the door came again.

"Yes, come in."

My dad opened the door. His bulk covered the doorframe. When I saw his eyes, the glint in them, I knew Aunty Damaris and the maid had rat me out. Those snitches!

"Bring the clothes and the shoes with you when you are coming."

He closed the door and laughed hysterically.

There was no koboko on the ground when I went to the living room. No water, pepper, chain, or rope; nothing to show he wanted to do his usual.

"Drop them there." He pointed to the spot close to the shelf.

"I was told you desperately want to go to that dinner party of yours. Is that so?"

"Yes, sir."

The uncertainty of what he would do to me was scarier than the whip and pepper. My insides were quaking.

"Come sit down here on the ground."

I dawdled toward him. I sat at his foot, between his legs, the same way I used to with Granny. From nowhere, Aunty Amara and Aunty Damaris came out. Aunty Damaris was holding a bowl filled with water, while the maid was with a towel.

"We would be giving your hair a treat," Dad said sadistically. "We don't want you going to such a party with a bad-looking hair. Dad tightened his legs around my waist. He pressed me down on my shoulder. Before that, though, he had instructed me to stay still. He didn't need a rope or handcuffs, fear kept me still. I slithered into the dark room filled with nails. It was over.

They cut my hair till I was bald. I sat there and allowed them cut off every chance of me attending the dinner. The awards I was supposed to collect, the dance I was supposed to have with my friends, the last ray of hope that I was looking forward to, they cut it off, stole it from me, and they relished the moment. Dad gave me back my clothes and shoes and told me, with an evil smirk on his face, that I could go to the party if I still wanted to. I dragged my feet to my room, tears streaming down my cheeks at their own accord. The splotches of blood on my bald head didn't hurt as much as my pride. My dad had finally won the battle to destroy my self-esteem. He had shattered it into unrecognizable splinters.

My WAEC result was released three weeks after, and I passed well. I had three As, four Bs, and two Cs. I wasn't the best in my school, but I came a close second to the girl who had four As, two Bs, and three Cs. Shina came to the house to give me the news. I wasn't happy at first, but when Shina told me that I could finally leave the hellhole of a house, I saw the light at the end of the dark and airless tunnel.

I told Dad about the result and how I needed money to get a JAMB (an examination taken by secondary school graduates to gain admission into tertiary institutions in Nigeria) form. He congratulated himself for my WAEC result. He said his discipline was paying off. But then after he had finish boasting of how he has successfully raised a good and respectful daughter (read depressed and broken and dead inside), he said he didn't have money to send me to university. I wanted to study mass communications at the university. I should hold on for one year, he said. He was short of cash, he told me. I should spend the next year with his wife. At least I would help her more at her store and take care of my brothers.

That one year at home, jobless, with nowhere to go, remains the darkest year in my life. Recounting the number of times I stayed hungry because my aunty and the maid thought I didn't need food, or the number of times the pepper-and-koboko-and-dog-chain treatment was administered to me, or the number of times my father dragged my naked body around the street, recounting these things and the scars it created only makes me cry even more. One year is more than enough time to see the devil face-to-face.

Finally

It started with mood swings. There were days where I was so excited and involved in school activities, I lit up every room I walked into. I was the life of the party and the perfect example my instructors used when they spoke to new students at orientation. New students would walk up to me to ask me to mentor them. I worked so hard because I didn't want to fail. Failure would mean going back to my father's house, and I dreaded that.

Then there were days when I couldn't get myself out of bed. I became obsessed with Jack Daniel's whisky. The spirits loved me, and I obliged them. With every sip, our bond got stronger. It was my escape from the past that I couldn't share. My friends didn't understand it when they saw this side of me. They called it scoin scoin. They wondered why I had these episodes, why I forgot things sometimes, and why I would get sad and withdraw from everyone and everything. They wondered why I cut myself. It didn't make any sense to them because I was a model student and so many other students looked up to me. The answers came in my junior year.

I was diagnosed with bipolar disorder and depression. My roommate Minna could not make sense out of any of this. She spent hours on the phone every day with someone who made her laugh and giggle so hard. Her phone beeped at about 5:00 p.m. every day, and Minna won't miss that call for anything in the world. She starts off with a greeting, then she starts talking about everything she did since she got out of bed. Listening to her conversations was always fun.

She would narrate all the interesting things she did, including the meals she had, then she would report some of her annoying professors and lazy class group members. She would rant about being forced to do group projects and so many other school affairs. For the last five minutes of the conversation, she would be quiet, listening as though she is taking notes. I'm guessing that's when she got advice. Then she would conclude with a thank -you, I love you, and I can't imagine a life without you. I found out that this person Minna spoke with every day like a ritual was her father. I was so jealous when she shared the information. I wanted to be in her shoes so bad. I wanted her daddy. I wanted her life. I wanted her happiness.

I finally shared my story with Minna. Now she knows why I behaved differently. A few weeks after I shared my story with Minna, she embarked on a research to find out if "traumatic events caused mental illness." I thought she was joking until she invited me to her class presentation. She found out that according to the World Health Organization, child maltreatment could aggravate lifelong physical and mental health challenges and that the emotional and social effects can eventually slow a country's economic and social development. Minna wanted to be my voice so bad. She became an advocate against physical abuse disguised as discipline. We had become soul sisters. She feels responsible for me, and my happiness has become her priority.

Living in a home where your body is not seen as a thing to be respected makes you believe that pain is the only way to find meaning. The constant discipline I received—and that Ibinabo and Jack received—from people who were supposed to protect us turned my body to a mass of slobbering fear. I am always looking over my shoulders, afraid that the next man walking beside me wanted to inflict pain. It is as if I lost all rights to my own flesh, as if my flesh is meant to be beaten and treated whatever way the oppressors choose.

I have no idea where Jack is or if he is still alive (I think Jack is still well and good, doing well for himself), but I know Ibinabo has been fine. She writes to me often and sometimes calls me. She was doing well with her fashion business. She told me the one time we spoke. She was planning on opening her own fashion school in her town.

I sometimes go to visit Grandma and Grandpa in the village. They are getting older and weaker, but Grandma's love for me is still as fresh as the morning dew. She still buys me Fanta and bole whenever I visit her. She assures me my mother is ready to see me whenever I am ready. I am not sure if I will ever be ready. I choose to not write about the content of Grandma's letter because the pages would not do. The things I found out later, mostly from Grandma are not what blockbuster movies are made of. Another book, another story. "But she is fine," Grandma says. She would love to introduce me to her new family whenever I was ready.

Dakumo is now studying in Finland. She got a scholarship to study creative arts. She is a painter. She didn't tell her mother about her scholarship. She told me on Facebook Messenger. She was scared they would do their juju to stop her from going.

"But you dey Lagos that time, why you dey fear juju from village?" I asked her. I was in my room trying to complete a Virginia Wolfe novel, *A Room of One's Own*.

"I like to respect me" was her apt response. She still queries me about the toys I promised her then. I told her that whenever she was in the country, she and I would get the Barbie dolls. I miss her madness.

I, too, have had my own fair share of fear-induced worthlessness, but each day, I struggled to find my worth in the things I am able to do. I have scars—just like my cousins—that remind me every single passing day just how much I was never my own. These scars remind me of how many people's bodies have lost their autonomy because they have parents, parents whose definition of discipline borders around the lines of excessive physical and mental abuse. It is never a good thing when I take a walk down memory lane. I still feel the whip on my body. I can still see the fire in his eyes when he raises his hand to correct me. And you know what is weird? I don't hate him for it. I don't think I'll ever be able to hate him the way I used to. I know better now. As much I wish he treated my cousins and I differently, I still love him.

Growing up, I have come to understand that love isn't linear. That love isn't something that can be logically explained with some random theories whipped out of thin air. Or one that has been systematically understood. You can't really understand love. And that is a fact.

He loved us, no matter how bizarre it sounds now. I know he loved us. He still calls me to know how I am doing and if I need anything. He doesn't sound like a man who would have acted differently because to him, he loved me the best way he knew how to.

I only hoped that the way he chose to express his love was different. I am seated here in my room, staring at the ticking clock and listening to the humming air conditioner, wishing that my dad, and all the generations who learned that love is *hard knocks*, would unlearn it. They would learn the new and accurate language of love: compassion.

Is it any fault of theirs? Not so much. Do I judge them? Not really.

I have a three-year-old child in my compound. There are days when she acts all three-year-oldy, and I want to smack her for doing something stupid. Instincts. I find myself holding back hurtful words whenever she refuses to stop playing with sand. I want to tell her all the nasty things inside me, but I restrain myself. I haven't always been successful. Sometimes the words slip out of my mouth, and I quickly apologize to her before the words become seeds in her heart. I am quick with an apology because I don't want her to learn the false language of love I was taught.

Knowing what I know now, one would think I would be all perfect and loving and caring and all those mushy things we know love to be. But I'm not. My past still finds a way to creep up on me, the same way it did on my dad.

My dad didn't know a different and better love language. In his bid to set things straight—as he was taught—he almost sent us skidding off the beautiful path he envisioned for us. He was ignorant of a different way of showing love, so he showed us *love* the only way he knew.

I hope, for the sake of my dad and other parents out there who were taught the distorted dialect of love as pain, that they relearn love. I hope they take time to be less authoritarian and more human. I hope they read books to help them better understand what love and parenting should be like, taking into cognizance their children's individual differences.

Will the journey to unlearning old habits be comfortable? Not in any way. But I am hoping that they don't continue loving their children and showing it in ways that turn their children into forgotten cities and war-ravaged cathedrals. I hope they learn that love smiles. That love hugs children. That love can be both gentle and firm without breaking walls and tearing skins and breaking the faucet of tears. That love is meek and mild while still being true to values. This way, when children grow up, they won't be emotionally detached from their parents and staying connected, or visiting home won't feel like a dreaded chore.

The scars that once defined me, that once haunted me, have now become my roadmap to becoming a better person. I am more empathic. I am learning to love myself like I am the goddess Athena. I am learning, with each trial and failure, to rewrite my broken story and make a collage of beautiful memories. I am learning, healing, and moving forward. I will break the cycle!

about the author

....

Blessing Douglas lives in Wheaton, Maryland. She had spent most of her life in Nigeria, her home country, but moved to the United States for graduate studies and career advancement. When she's not journaling her experiences, you might find Blessing Douglas volunteering at refugee camps, participating in mental health advocacy, which is one of her passions, or hosting leadership workshops for youths in her local commu-  nity. During her years of volunteering in college, Blessing Douglas found herself increasingly obsessed with the stories of people in the communities she served. Stories of domestic violence, child abuse, and mental illness, coupled with some of her personal experience, inspired her to work on the novel swimming around her head. Blessing hopes that her novel will provoke conversations about discipline and abuse where parents and caregivers cross the line, the psychological long-term effect on children's mental health as they grow into adulthood, a new orientation, and an awakening to learn, do better, and break the cycle of dysfunction.

CPSIA information can be obtained
at www.ICGtesting.com
Printed in the USA
LVHW112141200521
687738LV00021B/187

9 781649 520463